He stared at her with superb green eyes the color of a calm sea, but it was his slow smile that pierced her heart. Eyes and smile. Together they pulled her into the deep waters of wild imagination. The six-footer awkwardly tugged on his collar and no wonder, he seemed totally out of place at the theater's cast party. Ivy Dillon was ripe for romance. She had to meet *Whatzhisname.*

Wildcard

by

Robin Shope

This is a work of fiction. Names, characters, places, and incidents are either the product of the author's imagination or are used fictitiously, and any resemblance to actual persons living or dead, business establishments, events, or locales, is entirely coincidental.

Wildcard

Contact Information: info@thewildrosepress.com

Cover Art by *Kim Mendoza*

The Wild Rose Press
PO Box 708
Adams Basin, NY 14410-0706
Visit us at www.thewildrosepress.com

Publishing History
First Crimson Rose Edition, 2008
Print ISBN 1-60154-487-1

Published in the United States of America

Dedication

For Janet Shope
My critique partner & friend.
Thank you for your many hours of reading,
for your tips of wisdom and for your prayers.
You always knew that God
has something special planned.

Chapter One

He stared at her with superb green eyes the color of a calm sea, but it was his slow smile that pierced her heart. Eyes and smile. Together they pulled her into the deep waters of wild imagination. The six-footer awkwardly tugged on his collar and no wonder, he seemed totally out of place at the theater's cast party. Ivy Dillon was ripe for romance. She had to meet *Whatzhisname.*

"Here's your fruit punch." Jordan nudged. "I snagged you a cup before the alcohol went in."

"Thanks." Ivy turned toward her roommate. "By the way, who's that?"

"Who?"

"The great looking guy near the window." Ivy tipped her head in that direction.

"You can't mean Martin?" Jordan snorted.

"Martin?" Ivy whipped around and squinted. Sure enough, the man she set her sights on meeting had disappeared and in his place was Martin, in drag, wearing evening gown garb and full makeup. He waved at her. Ivy waved back, disappointedly. "No, not him."

Ivy cruised through the stage director's apartment, trying to catch sight of the man with the interesting angular features, the hair that curled up along his neckline, and, oh yes, those eyes—those amazing eyes.

On her way by the dessert table, the chocolate covered strawberries distracted her. She bit into one, enjoying the meeting of two rivers of flavors, and just like that Whatzhisname appeared in front of her. Magic!

"You have a bit of chocolate right there," he told her pointing at the corner of her mouth.

"Thanks," Ivy croaked.

"May I?" he asked permission to touch her skin and wipe the chocolate away.

Ivy moved closer and felt the gentle stroke of his touch. Just like strawberries and chocolate, Ivy knew they were meant to be.

"There, you're perfect again." He licked his chocolate finger and then glanced around the room scanning faces. "Great opening night for the play. Do you know the cast?"

Ivy nodded. "Yes, in fact, the leading actress is my friend."

"Jordan Belle is your roommate? Interesting."

"How did you know she was my roommate?"

Just as Whatzhisname opened his mouth to answer, Martin swayed up and held out a platter of canapés. "Would you help pass these for me, doll?" he asked Ivy, blowing feathers back from his boa.

No, no, definitely no. No way did she want to do anything that would take her away from a promising evening. It was hard to resist the urge to shove the food back toward Martin's fake bosom. Politely, Ivy accepted the canapés and offered them to the guests. The next time she looked up Whatzhisname was heading toward the front door. Running after him would be way too pathetic so she let him go. She had to. He went one way and she went the other way to the balcony where she hoped to catch one last glimpse of him as he left the building. Ivy leaned over railing and waited. And waited.

An unexpected hand on her shoulder made her jump back, dropping her purse as she did so. The contents flew everywhere. "Oh no!" Ivy chased her belongings, hoping to save them before they rolled over the edge.

"Are you all right?" a male voice asked, as she saw hands scrambling to help pick up the loose items—lipstick, business cards, inhaler, loose change and billfold.

She looked into his face and sighed. "It's you!"

Whatzhisname was back, with the perfect stormy eyes and that slow smile. It was enough to melt the ice sculpture on the buffet table. She shivered with delight.

"I didn't mean to frighten you."

"You didn't frighten me."

"I hate to contradict you, but you looked quite frightened."

"Startled may be the more appropriate word choice, but I assure you that I ain't frightened," Ivy panned.

"Ain't ain't a word."

"I know. I used it for effect." She loved the color of his eyes.

"I guess that makes it all right then." One at a time, he handed back her items. However, he held tightly onto her business card. "Is this *your* card?"

"Yes, it is."

"Then I must keep it," he sweetly added as if he had no other desire than to know her.

Just like that, Ivy let him pull it from between her fingers. "I think I have everything now, thanks to you." She snapped her purse shut.

"That's good." He straightened, slipped the card into his jacket pocket and returned to the party.

His abrupt exit made Ivy dizzy. Nonchalantly, she strolled though the party, smiling and nodding at the guests hoping to find Whatzhisname again. She had a dozen things she wanted to know about him, among them his name. However, they all drained from her head when Jordan hooked her by the arm.

"Catch a cab home. I'll see ya in the morning." With the toss of her long hair, Jordan skipped out of the party with a man on her arm.

Just then Whatzhisname sailed right on by as he headed out the front door, without even so much as a goodbye. Her window of opportunity had shut. After a few more chocolate covered strawberries eaten over deep sighs, it was Ivy's turn to go home.

****

Ivy sat at the end of the pier with her feet in the water. She stared up at the oversized moon. The reflection of the heavenly constellation floated across the bay toward the shore on a parade of ripples. Suddenly, they turned into hands and leapt toward her, cold wet fingers wrapped around her ankles. With a jerk, she was pulled beneath the lake. Frantically, she fought to free herself but she was no match. She lay motionless at the sandy bottom. Something poked her. Slowly, Ivy opened her eyes and inches away lay a body with hair swirling around the head. A skeleton hand reached out to her.

A dog howled outside on Washington Street.

Ivy bolted straight up in bed and pulled at the constricting button on the neck of her nightgown. She couldn't breathe. Mechanically, she swung her arm toward her prescription inhaler and accidentally propelled it across the room. It smacked the wall and hit the floor.

She knew it would be impossible to find her inhaler in a room draped in shadows so she staggered to the window and yanked open the shade. With daylight now sparkling on the floor, she turned to find her inhaler on its side beneath the green cushioned chair alongside her bed. She dropped to her knees and snatched it. Ivy rocked back on her heels and opened her mouth. Several blasts of medicine sprayed her throat, allowing air to rush into her lungs. Slowly, she counted her breaths as her eyes settled on a single rosebud in the pattern of her curtains. Bit by bit, she recovered.

Now all she wanted to do was fall back into bed, drag the blanket over her head and sleep for ten hours. Instead, she mustered her strength and latched onto the arm of the chair to pull up. It didn't matter how sick she felt, she had to go to work.

She took off her nightgown and tuned the radio to a news talk station. Two political analysts from opposing parties were doing what they did best—arguing.

"Slow down, men," she told them on the way into the bathroom. "The next presidential election is still two years away."

Ivy stepped into the shower. The whoosh of the water in her face resurfaced the nightmare of the moonlight, the fingers, and the feeling of not being able to breathe. Ten years later and she was still haunted by finding her best friend dead in the lake shallows. She felt thankful that during the day she skated above the thoughts, but sometimes at night, when her defenses were down, they returned. Ivy shut her eyes tighter but the memory of Karin's pale skin and dead eyes was all she could see. It weighed her down making her weak with terror. Ivy leaned against the tiles until she regained her balance.

The phone rang. Ivy didn't move. On the third ring, she reached out for the knob and shut off the stream of water. After she slipped into her robe, she made her way to the phone. The Caller ID read anonymous. She shouldn't answer, she knew this, but she couldn't stop herself. Her hands shook as she picked up the receiver. "Hello?"

"Erin, thank goodness I finally found you." As usual the 'Voice' was calm, so in control.

"No one by that name lives here," Ivy pushed out the words in a whisper and then slammed down the phone. She waited for it to ring again since it always did. The sound of his creepy tenor seemed to drip from the bathroom walls. Ivy kept staring at the phone, trembling. This time, there was no second call.

Now all Ivy wanted was to get out of the apartment and on the street where she felt safer and not so isolated. In her hurry, she nearly broke the zipper on her skirt as she struggled to get dressed.

Then, just as she reached the door, she heard someone fiddling with the doorknob. Ivy set her briefcase and purse down and peered through the peephole. In the hallway was the unmistakable form of her roommate who was now digging through her bag. Ivy turned the lock on the door and Jordan sailed into the apartment.

"Thank goodness you're still here. I can't find my key again."

"It's lucky you caught me. Another minute and I'd be gone."

Jordan hugged several copies of the theater critic's section to her chest. "Do you have time to read my reviews before you leave?"

"I always have time for you." Ivy took a paper and read the metro section. "*Jordan Belle Stands Out Among a Talented Cast.* The only way it could get better is if people knew who you really were, Erin Lowe."

"My theater name is Jordan Belle. Never, ever refer to me using my given name again."

"What's the harm? There's only the two of us here."

"Because you might slip up when it really matters," Jordan said dramatically with a lift of an eyebrow.

"I can't shake the feeling that there is something more you are not telling me." Frustrated, Ivy needed to know. "What is it?"

Jordan bit her lip.

"Jordan, we've been through a lot since your sister Karin's death. You owe it to me to let me know what it is you're hiding from. Help me to understand."

Jordan dropped into a chair, crossing one leg over the other. "All you need to know is that it involves the 'Voice'. As long as he can't find me, I'll be happy."

"Well, Jordan Belle, prepare to be sad. The 'Voice' called this morning asking for Erin."

Chapter Two

Seven fifty nine. Ivy passed through the west-wing corridor. The senior guard greeted her with his one-hundred-kilowatt smile. Gus was near retirement and counting down the days until he moved to Louisiana to open a small eatery in New Orleans. A crown of silver hair framed his lined face. "Good morning, Ms. Dillon."

"Morning, Gus." She smiled back, holding up her "Washington Intern" badge and then placed her purse, briefcase and both shoes on the x-ray belt.

"What no sandwich today?" he teased, watching the monitor.

"No, not today. Today, I have plans for lunch."

"Anyone I know?"

"You might. He's very famous," Ivy answered, putting one shoe back on and then the other. "How many days until you swap your gun for a spatula?"

"Ten, counting today. Come and visit me. I'll cook us up some Jambalaya with red beans and rice that will spoil you for anything else."

"Sounds yummy. I may just do that." Ivy winked at him and then picked up her belongings.

As the intern to President Harris's personal secretary, Ms. Geneen Waters, her job translated into spending copious amounts of time photocopying and preparing conference rooms for meetings.

"You're here early *again*, Miss Dillon," Ms. Waters noted.

"Since my internship is over at the end of the week, I want my work done."

Ms. Waters wore a business gray dress-suit with a pink organdy blouse. As usual, her hair was styled in a tight knot with wisps of wiry black hair coming free. An attractive, elderly black woman, she carried herself with classic dignity on one-inch chunky heels. "You are exemplary. Please use my name for a reference."

"I am honored. Your name will sure impress everyone." Ivy returned to her work and her morning was filled with phone calls. Midmorning, Ivy checked her wristwatch. "Lunchtime. Today, I'm getting a hot dog from the stand across the street."

"What a perfect day to eat in the park." Ms. Waters glanced out the window at the myriad of cherry trees in blossom.

"It is, but I'll be eating on the fly while on my way to the bookstore. Today is the release date for my favorite author's newest book and I want to pick it up. I teased Gus that I was having lunch with someone famous." Ivy pulled her purse from the bottom desk drawer. "I can devour his thrillers in a single weekend."

"I never figured you to be interested in reading about crime." Ms. Waters sounded disappointed in Ivy's selection.

"What's your favorite genre?"

"Romance!"

"Really? I can't bring myself to read one completely through. I mean, what's the point? Woman pines for the man, woman cries. Woman thinks about the man, watches the man, and then finally gets the man. No surprise there. I never was one for romance." Ivy crossed to the elevator and then turned to ask, "May I get anything for you while I'm out?"

"Yes, if you don't mind, I need Time magazine."

"Time magazine," Ivy repeated as the private elevator doors opened and two congressmen stepped out into the foyer. "Will do."

"But it has to be last month's issue," Ms. Waters emphasized. She walked to Ivy digging through her purse. Taking a five-dollar bill from her billfold, she spoke in a low voice, "There is a particular article in it about Trojan horses. Be sure to get the correct issue."

Outside, the pollen made Ivy wheeze. She used her inhaler and then crossed the street to a vendor selling hot dogs. After piling the bun with relish and ketchup, she took big bites, easily finishing it off. Ivy wiped her mouth and hands before tossing her trash into a bin by the door to the bookstore.

It was the first release day of many popular authors, which explained why the place was packed. Right there on the first table near the entrance was what she had planned on purchasing.

"You're the only man I know who promises excitement and actually delivers it," she murmured to the author's picture on the back cover. Ivy tucked the book under her arm and then headed to the magazine rack. There wasn't a single copy of last month's issue of Time. They were all current.

The line to the fifth cashier was thinning. Ivy started walking that way when she saw him; it was just a profile but one she could never forget. It made her take a second look. The third time she downright stared at him.

Sam Oliver, her former fiancé, was heading directly her way. If she didn't do something fast, they'd be face-to-face, nose-to-nose. Quickly, Ivy spun around and snatched a magazine off the shelf. It turned out to be a Bride's magazine. The bride on the cover seemed to mock her; Ivy returned the magazine to the shelf by placing it upside down.

It wasn't until Sam brushed past her that she dared to take her next breath. Like a snoop, Ivy followed Sam to the children's section that was decked out in larger-than-life cartoonish cutouts, mini-tables and chairs. Ivy remained lurking in the teacher's resource section, between the thesauruses and grammar textbooks. Sam sat down with a little boy and they paged through a children's book. As Sam read the words, the little boy laughed. A hot dog lump formed in the middle of her stomach.

Minutes later a woman joined the pair. Ivy guessed her to be his wife as Sam rose to greet her. "I'll take those for you, hon." She handed him the children's books and he kissed her cheek. Yes, that was his wife all right. *Sometimes in life one gets lucky.*

All three of them walked her way. Of course they would since she stood between them and the cashier. Ivy did an about-face and headed down the non-fiction section. She hid behind a stack of board games and waited for the Olivers to pass.

Positive she was now in the clear, Ivy turned and did a full body slam into Sam. The top of her head clipped his jawline and he stumbled into a shelf of thick collegiate dictionaries. It was enough to make any mortal man drop to his knees, but Sam, a former football star, was no ordinary man. He remained on his feet, albeit swaying a bit with a dazed expression. Sam's brow had taken the brunt of the hit, and fortunately, it made him squint. It was a relief that he didn't look at her but instead dropped to his knees and started picking up the books. His wife looked directly at Ivy and laughed.

"Sorry." Mrs. Oliver explained, "Sam never watches where he's going."

Ivy looked into Mrs. Oliver's eyes, wondering what kind of a woman snagged this wonderful guy. Hazel eyes sparkled back at her. Yes, Sam must've put the twinkle there.

"Can I help you, Miss?" the cashier at the front of the store impatiently signaled to Ivy.

"Changed my mind." Ivy pushed out through the heavy front glass doors, leaving her much anticipated book on the counter.

****

"Sorry..."

"They didn't have last month's issue of Time."

"Never mind," Ms. Waters stewed. "And where is your new book?"

"We both struck out." Ivy demurred with a lift of her shoulders. "If you need me, I'll be at the copy machine."

Ivy laid Ms. Waters' money on her desk as she headed down the hall to the copy room. Once there, Ivy slid the first of the originals into the top tray of the copier and pressed twenty copies to be collated and stapled. There were three more originals after this load to do. It was going to be a long afternoon, so she plugged in earphones to practice her French. She wanted to be proficient in the language when she visited France someday.

"*Enchant*e," she whispered. Just as the last job finished, the iPod stopped playing. It was dead. For now she left her earphones in as she stacked the materials on a pushcart and began her deliveries. Reading down her list, she counted out ten booklets for the conference room.

As she picked up the packets, the earplugs fell out and now were hanging around her ankles like miniature bungee cords. Ivy tried to ignore them but when she stepped forward they wrapped around her legs, making her trip. She dropped her armload. Ivy groaned. Now most of the packets were damaged and would have to be redone. As Ivy squatted down to collect them, she only heard bits and pieces of the conversation between the two men in the conference room. Ivy struggled to keep up with their exchange.

"Look on the bright side...there's only three, maybe four, of us who are privy to the *entire* plan so...from us—you, me, and the Top Dog Boss."

"Don't forget about the last one."

"Has Top Dog located the woman yet?"

"It's been blackout silence...never mind about her, just give me twenty-four hours to get what we need. Regard it as a misplacement of the files."

"Did you say *misplacement* of files? Does that include our timeline *plans* and the code combinations?"

"Ah, yea, I'm afraid it does. The package was together...missing."

"Missing? They're crucial! We've been planning this for years and now just when we are so close to winning the White House, and both houses, you..."

One of the men began coughing and his voice trembled a bit. "You might as well know...I can't find the prototype microchip either."

"I'm panicking here..." A fist hit the wall.

"Please don't tell me you'll...later. You were to look them over and then turn them in to me. You must grasp the enormity of this! It not only affects the next election but the line-up of candidates from both sides...short window of opportunity and...closing. We can't do this without the mainframe codes and the microchip...we should have made copies."

"Do me a favor. Don't let Top Dog Boss know yet, okay? Give me a few days."

"By then, you had better have your hands on the entire project or...our time schedule...costing us another election. Without the package and hard drive, it's an avalanche just waiting to roar down a political mountain."

"I had it all together in a large brown envelope and it was right in my hand. I was...the combination on the wall safe when Ms. Waters walked in saying President Harris needed to see me immediately. You don't keep the President of the United States waiting, or Ms. Waters for that matter. When I got back, it was gone."

"Why didn't you just put them into the wall safe when Ms. Waters walked in? What would a few more minutes have mattered?"

"I thought locking my office door would be enough."

"There you go thinking again! Follow orders instead."

Ivy sat back on her heels and looked around. There was a piece of paper lodged halfway under one of the fat wheels. She pulled it. Pulled it again, and then once more. To her horror, this time the wheel squeaked.

"Ivy!" Ms Waters stood over her.

"Yes, ma'am?"

"Clean up your mess and leave this area immediately. Obviously, those bundles need to be redone and I need them quickly."

The tone of Ms. Waters' voice was out of character. Whatever they had overheard, whatever it meant, suddenly seemed threatening to her. Ivy wanted to ask Ms. Waters but decided against it. The best thing she could do was follow her mentor's instructions and keep quiet.

Chapter Three

The lock on her apartment door had been broken.

"Jordan?" Ivy called. She stood in the threshold and peered into the living room. Pictures were yanked down from the walls, white tufts of batting from pillows blew through the apartment on AC currents much like tumbleweeds; cabinets were open revealing spilled contents.

"Jordan!" she called again but this time with greater urgency.

Not sure it was safe to enter, Ivy backed out of the residence. She pounded on the neighbor's door across the way to ask if she could use their phone. No answer. Ivy pounded on another door but again no answer.

Frantic, she looked around. Maybe someone would be home upstairs. She held onto the banister and ran up the flight. There, at the top, a door was slightly ajar. A light was on in the room.

"Please help me!" she called to the man sitting in the armchair.

He stood and turned around. One look at Ivy and a cocky-feel-good smile spread across his face.

He took off his glasses and set them on a table. "What's wrong, you look frightened."

The sight of Whatzhisname made her falter. "Um, my apartment has been burgled! I need to call my roommate Erin to be sure she's all right."

"I thought your roommate was Jordan Belle?"

"Oh, pardon me." Ivy couldn't believe she slipped

so easily. "I meant to say Jordan. I need to be sure she's still at the theater and not…"

Whatzhisname handed her his phone.

With nervous fingers, Ivy called Jordan's cell. *Please pick up. Please be all right.*

"Hello, this is Martin."

"Martin, it's Ivy—"

"Hello, dolllink, Ivy," he answered for her dramatically.

"Martin! Is Jordan there? I really need to talk to her."

"Slow down, will you? Of course, she's here. In fact, I'm standing in the wings and can see her right now on stage. What's wrong?"

"Tell her to give me a call before she leaves for home. Can you remember that?"

"I think I am able to remember that," he answered with irritation.

"I'm sorry; I didn't mean to sound condescending."

"Too late." Martin hung up.

"Let me contact the police for you." Whatzhisname pulled his cell from her fingers. After the call was placed, Ivy started to leave.

"Wait," he warned her. "There might still be someone in your apartment. It's safer to stay here with me until the police arrive."

"I planned on waiting outside for them."

"Then I'll come with you." He slid his stocking feet into shoes and followed her to the stoop where they sat watching for the police to show. "Ivy, I'm glad I was home when you needed someone. I can't imagine how frightening it would be to walk into a ransacked apartment but you're safe now as there is strength in numbers."

"I'm glad you were home, too." She smiled up at him.

Whatzhisname scooted closer and enveloped her

hand in his. The gesture was small but made Ivy feel totally protected from any harm that might come her way. She stared at his profile as he watched the street. He had a strong jawline.

He must have sensed her stare because he looked at her with his piercing green eyes and smiled. "You'll be just fine, trust me."

"I do."

It took the police twenty minutes to arrive. By now, as far as Ivy was concerned, they could have taken all night, but such was not her luck. Two male cops got out of the squad car and came up the walkway where they waited on the stoop.

"We got a call about a burglary."

"Yes, my place was broken into sometime today while I was at work." Ivy led the way into her apartment while Whatzhisname continued up to his floor closing his door quietly.

The police went through all the rooms as Ivy followed along, naming what was missing. Everything valuable had been taken—her laptop computer, TV and radio. Before they left, the phone started to ring and the shrill sound caused chills to run over Ivy's skin. The last thing she needed was to listen to the troubling taunts of the 'Voice'.

"Aren't you going to answer it?" one of the cops asked, looking from Ivy to the phone and back again.

Ivy looked at the Caller ID. It read *Anonymous*. No way would she deal with the 'Voice' now so she shook her head. "It can wait. I need to finish reading through your police report." The phone abruptly stopped in the middle of the fourth ring. Ivy signed the statement, fairly certain her items would never be recovered. The police were gone only minutes when the phone rang for the second time. Again the Caller ID read *Anonymous*.

Her heart rate doubled. Ivy stood over the landline waiting for it to stop. She gave herself permission not to answer it. She could out wait the caller, but then it occurred to her that it might not be the 'Voice' after all. Maybe someone, like Martin, from the theater was calling to say Jordan had stumbled off the edge of the stage during her performance. It could even be Jordan returning her phone call during intermission. What if it was Whatzhisname from upstairs inviting her up for a drink to calm her nerves? She didn't drink alcohol but he didn't know that. Phones were installed for a purpose. Not everyone abused them.

"Hello?" Ivy finally answered on the sixth ring

"Tell Erin, now that I have found her again, rest assured I won't ever let her out of my sight. I will dog her footsteps day and night until..." The 'Voice' continued talking but Ivy stopped listening. She yanked the cord from the wall, grabbed her purse and ran out of the apartment. Ivy jogged for a few blocks before she stopped. A Chinese diner was the only place still open in the neighborhood. She went inside and soon sat over a plate of egg foo young. She took her time eating but began to notice the owner cleaning the place around her. She was the only one left and the last thing she wanted to do was return to her apartment. Ivy ordered a second meal to go before they closed.

Whatzhisname had been so comforting that she wanted to thank him with the dinner. If he saw how jittery she still was, maybe he'd invite her in for a while. Ivy darted past her apartment door and scooted up the flight of stairs. It was after ten but she took a gamble and knocked. In seconds, there he stood—all six feet of him.

"Ivy, are you all right?" he stepped back as she bolted past him into his place.

She handed him the dinner. "Thank you for earlier this evening. I don't know what I would have done without you."

"You didn't need to gift me with dinner; it was my pleasure to help."

"It's the 'Happy Family Dinner Special'." Ivy blinked up at him. "There are fortune cookies, too." Ivy handed him the brown paper bag.

"It looks to me as though you might need someone to talk to," he set the bag on the table.

"Do you mind if that someone is you?"

"Not at all. Sit and I'll get us a couple of plates." He pointed at a dining room chair and placed the dishes on the table next to the large carton of Chinese food and handful of fortune cookies. He filled two glasses with water, added lemon and ice and set one glass in front of her and the other in front of his place.

Ivy looked around at the sparse furnishings. "Are you in the process of just moving in or moving out?"

"I travel lightly," he explained. Then he slid a fortune cookie across the table to her. "Here, you go first."

Ivy unwrapped it and broke it open. She read, "'Man's schemes are inferior to those made in heaven'. Interesting."

"Now it's my turn." Whatzhisname made his selection and broke his cookie open. "'Pick the flower when it is ready to be picked'." He looked into Ivy's eyes making her blush. His smile was the perfect medicine for anything. "I guess there are several ways that saying can be interpreted. Who gets a job writing fortune cookies, anyway?"

"I agree; how *do* you find out about an opening for such a career move." Ivy shrugged with a lift of her shoulders.

"I wonder if it's a new college major." Whatzhisname spooned the food from the carton onto their plates.

"Maybe that could be my next career move."

Ivy's sudden laughter surprised her.

"You have a nice laugh."

"After the day I've had, it feels good to laugh." For several minutes, it was quiet as Ivy moved noodles and bits of pepper around with her fork. She sensed he was waiting for her to talk but now she felt at a loss for words.

Whatzhisname had all ready worked his way through half his Chinese dish. He looked at her and narrowed his eyes as if trying to read her. Setting his fork at the edge of his plate, he gently said, "I'm here and I'll listen if you want to talk."

"It's late and I should leave. There must be things you need to do. Like getting a good night's sleep for one thing." Ivy looked down at the folded napkin on her lap. "But I don't want to go back to my apartment. Not yet."

"Then stay, Ivy. I'm all yours. Talk to me." He pushed back his plate along with the remaining cookies and leaned over the table waiting for her to speak. When she didn't, he kicked off the conversation. "I imagine you were cleaned out."

"Yes, but I didn't have much to begin with. What little there was is now gone. It took me months to save for my laptop!" Ivy hit the table with her open hand. "It's been taken along with other things…like the feeling of safety."

"And?" he prodded

"After the police left, I got this creepy phone call." Ivy explained.

"Oh? Burglars usually don't call their victims."

"Separate incident." She looked up at him through her eyelashes.

"Sorry, I didn't mean to minimize. You've had two terrible events in one evening." Whatzhisname agreed. "Do you want to tell me about the call?"

"My roommate and I have been getting them for a while." Ivy stopped short. If she said anything more then she'd have to tell him the entire story of Erin living under an assumed name. She didn't want to go there.

"Any idea who they're from?"

"No, but I do know that he either needs therapy or a new hobby."

"At least you haven't lost your sense of humor," he guffawed. "Do you have Caller ID? Or tried pressing *69?"

"Yes, and neither gives any information. We've moved a few times and even changed our number but the 'Voice' tracks us down. He always asks for my roommate and she refuses to go to the phone."

"It sounds to me as though it could be a former boyfriend who can't take no for an answer." He raised an eyebrow.

"I was just wondering the same thing. Thanks for putting it into perspective."

"Talking things out can be helpful."

"You're the first man who's ever been interested in listening to my feelings," Ivy said. "You're a rare species."

"I can't imagine any man not wanting to listen to an intelligent and beautiful woman such as yourself. This has been nice for me."

"You're girlfriend is very blessed." Ivy fished hoping he was available.

"I travel a lot and don't have time for any relationship at this time in my life." Whatzhisname picked up the plates and carried them to the sink.

Ivy picked up the gooey empty carton along with the silverware and set them on the counter. "What do you do for a living?"

They heard hammering on the floor below and walked out into the hall where they looked over the banister to see the building super installing a new lock for Ivy. "Oh good. I feel so much better now." She breathed a deep sigh of relief.

"Is that you, Ivy Dillon?" The super looked up the stairs at them. "I fixed the doorjamb and have the key for your new lock."

"I'll be right down!" Ivy called. "I guess I better go. Maybe we can continue with this conversation another time."

"I'd like that, but for now try to get some sleep." He touched her face.

Ivy nodded in agreement and started down the steps.

"If something else unsettling happens, I'm right here tonight, okay?" He gave her a smile of compassion.

"Okay."

"Hey, I'll check on you in the morning." His voice followed her.

She turned around and waved. "I look forward to it."

After she got the key from the super, and was tucked safely behind the new lock, she called Jordan again. "But the police were here and I cleaned up the mess," Ivy tried to hide the fear in her voice.

"No way am I going back there tonight. You shouldn't stay either. Let's get a hotel room, or we can stay here at Martin's."

It was safe here now with Whatzhisname only steps away. Besides he was going to check on her in the morning. "I'll be just fine right here."

"Listen, Martin and I are on our way to pick you up."

"That isn't necessary. The super was up here already and the lock is fixed. Everything the burglars wanted is now in their possession so they won't be back. Besides, I'll sleep better in my own bed tonight."

"Okay, but call if you change your mind."

"I will but don't count on hearing from me. The safest place in the world is right here." Ivy smiled as she looked up at the ceiling with thoughts of Whatzhisname abounding.

Man, I can't believe I forgot to ask him his name—again.

****

The sun had been up for hours.

It was way past time to leave for work but Ivy lingered waiting to be checked on by her handsome rescuer. She sat on the couch, watching the clock, while wearing her favorite navy-blue dress with a fluted skirt. As if she wasn't nervous enough, the phone starting to ring added to it. Upon checking the ID, she found that *Anonymous* was trying to stir her up again but for once, he wasn't going to frighten her—not with Whatzhisname so close.

As the minutes ticked by, it became clear he wasn't coming after all. Filled with disappointment, Ivy left for work. After locking the apartment, she paused for a moment on the landing and stared up the stairway. In that moment, she decided to ask him out. The night before they had made a connection and her time in Washington was coming to a close. Time was a wasting. Up the flight of steps she went, her heart racing with anticipation and the usual stomach butterflies were fluttering.

The door was slightly ajar. Feeling effervescent with thoughts of him, she called, "Hello?"

When there was no response, she pushed the door open with sweaty palms. To her surprise, the apartment was empty. Even the chairs they had sat on and the table they ate at hours earlier were gone. Puzzled, Ivy slowly walked through the place and in every room she called out, "Hello?" Only the sound of her own voice greeted her.

Quickly, she pulled open every closet. Not even a hanger remained. In the bathroom she checked the medicine cabinet. Nothing. Why would someone move so completely in eight hours during the dead of night?

Next she headed for the kitchen to check the garbage. She yanked the bin out from under the sink. At the bottom of the trash, there was a single item left behind. The box of Chinese takeout. It intrigued her.

“Well at least I didn’t imagine the whole evening,” Ivy sighed with relief as she set the takeout on the counter. With nimble fingers, Ivy opened the lid and peered inside. The carton had been rinsed out and at the bottom was one fortune cookie, still wrapped in cellophane. It was too tempting to bypass so she tore off the wrapping and broke the cookie in two. The strip of paper read, *Good luck seldom comes in pairs but bad luck never walks alone.*

****

On top of her desk at work was a pink frosted cupcake.

Beside it was a wrapped gift from Ms Waters. “Ivy, I never married and now I live with my widowed sister. If I had married and was blessed enough to have a daughter, I hope she would be as fine and exemplary as you. Because of that, I want you to know that this is the first gift I’ve given to an intern, ever, and it’s from my personal library.” Mrs. Waters was standing beside the desk waiting for her to open it.

“I am humbled by your words.” Ivy opened the gift to find an antique book on Egyptian history, bound in leather. Stunned, she slowly paged through it. The leather had deepened in color and cracked a bit while some of the gold lettering had flaked away. The feel of its skin was worn as if dozens of hands had read through the pages. The printed words were small, followed by pictures, drawings and a few old maps.

“When we visited the Smithsonian together last

month for your birthday, I noticed how you enjoyed the ancient exhibits. Egypt happens to be one of my areas of interest so you can imagine how pleased I was when you displayed curiosity."

"Your passion was inspiring."

Seemingly pleased with her answer, Ms. Waters took another step closer. "The book includes a chapter about the first woman Pharaoh. She reminds me a bit of you. Against incredible odds, she became the first woman Pharaoh. In turn, Egypt became a prosperous nation for many centuries until the Romans came and conquered it, never regaining its former glory or influence in the world. However, to this day Hatshupset's most important shrine still stands. It has a gold tip to reflect the rising sun in the east. I even have a picture of that monument in my home. Please promise to keep that book in a safe place. It may be worth the price of a king's ransom one day."

"I promise; I have something for you, too." Ivy pulled a small wrapped gift from her purse and handed it to Ms. Waters.

"I love this cologne; you have spent way too much on me!" Teary-eyed, Ms. Waters picked up her handbag and left for the ladies room just as the private line from the Oval Office buzzed. Ivy looked around. No one was in sight, so Ivy answered, "Hello, White House Intern Ivy Dillon speaking."

"Oh, goodie gun drops, Ms. Dillon, it's you; this is Michael Grayson."

She suppressed her giggle as she decided not to correct the second most powerful man of the free world by pointing out it's goodie *gum* drops not goodie *gun* drops. "Yes, Mr. Vice President, how may I help you?"

Chapter Four

Home again, home again in Twin Lakes, Wisconsin.

It was a beautiful hilly spot left behind by melting glaciers, the perfect mix of farming community and tourist retreat. Lake Mary, the shallower of the two lakes, was her home. Most of the businesses had gone sour so antique stores, overloaded with treasures from former times, moved into them. Nestled below the arms of tall oak trees, the houses were neatly kept up and were as individual as the people who lived inside of them. Ivy's house of worship, where she accepted Jesus as her savior at age fourteen, sat on Church Square.

The town was hemmed in by the rolling hills, where corn grew straight and tall in endless fields of thick leafy green. Songs of cicadas filled the air as dragonflies dipped their transparent wings in the spring-fed lake that cut deeply into the rich black soil and mayflies drove her close to insanity. Ivy thought it was the perfect place to live, that is, until she stumbled upon the body of Karin Lowe in the shallows. Now it was the last place she wanted to be. All her deepest fears seemed to sail back to her here, filling her sleep with nightmares. Ivy was anxious to head out of town.

Ivy's sandals smacked loudly going up the steps of the Twin Lakes Post Office. She passed her handful of resumes through the window to the postal worker. After buying more stamps, she slid them into the side pocket of her large, new handbag, a parting gift from Jordan a month earlier. On the way back down the steps, she noticed a black stretch limousine rolling down the street. She watched the limo pull to a stop in front of the café. Two men jumped out and opened the rear door for a tall, sandy-haired figure, dressed in style. He got out on the curb. Curious, Ivy followed them into the restaurant.

The locals had all the tables so Ivy took the only open seat at the counter. In nanoseconds, a couple of waitresses carried in a table for the official to sit at. Meanwhile, several of the locals got up to shake his hand. It was odd how his bodyguards allowed people to access their man so easily. At least a half dozen precautions needed immediate implementation.

An idea brewed in her head. Ivy started jotting down safety measures for improvement on her steno pad. Point by point, she addressed each concern. The proposal would look better formally typed out but there wasn't time and the opportunity sat a few yards away. A handwritten plan would have to do. It might be enough to get her an interview. Now she needed an opening, a way to get his attention but his face was hidden in a menu.

"May I help you, Ivy?" the waitress's voice loomed behind her. A gray-headed woman in her late fifties had even, sedate features. Her yellow uniform showed off a full, round figure. Serving pie all day sure had its perks. The tag pinned to her bosom was crooked and simply read 'Lucy'. Lucy set a glass of ice water down in front of Ivy.

"Who's that guy?" Ivy pushed back the glass of water a few inches.

"Oh, he's a congressman from Illinois." The waitress laid her order pad on the counter and perched a sharpened pencil on top.

"A congressman?" Only the president and vice president had secret service to protect them, so he had to have hired his own bodyguards, which explained the sloppiness. And he had an ego, which explained the limo.

"Everyone's wondering if he'll be running for a second term."

"Why is that?"

Taping her pencil excitedly, Lucy explained, "From what I catch in the news, he's had more than his share of problems during his first term. One of the biggest was the blackout in Des Plaines. It took days for all the lights to come back on."

"What caused it?" Ivy lowered her voice.

"Old grid. Needed updating."

"But that wasn't his fault."

"No, but tell that to the people who had a freezer full of spoiled meat in one hundred degree weather." She nodded as if this was the most horrible thing that could have happened to him. Poor congressman. "If he runs, it will be a close race."

"The congressman looks familiar." Ivy tried to remember.

"That's Congressman Robert Gram."

"*That's* Robert Gram?" Ivy gasped. "Do you know if he used to summer with his parents on the Wisconsin side of Twin Lakes?"

"Yes, indeedie."

Ivy clearly remembered her precarious date with him. Years had not erased the memory of fighting off the advances of the boy, and here sat the man. From what she witnessed that night, she thought he'd be a whiskey-soaked beach-bum by now.

"If you're going to sit here, you have to order food," Lucy said.

A figure in the wall mirror behind the counter caught Ivy's eye. In the far back booth sat a man with angular features, green eyes and a slow smile aimed in her direction. Whatzhisname saluted her. Miracles do happen. Ivy hopped off the stool but

Lucy reached over the counter and caught her arm. "What are you having?"

"A glass of orange juice and buttered wheat toast." Ivy jerked away, and with heart pounding optimism, hurried to find him but just like the apartment, the booth was empty. She had to find him. Ivy walked the floor of the café, searching for Whatzhisname. It caught Gram's eye. He nodded at her and she nodded back. He pointed to an empty chair across the table from him. "Join me?"

Ivy walked to Gram's table, wondering if Whatzhisname was a mirage. She dug out her expired Washington intern's badge and handed it to Congressman Gram.

"So you're a Washington intern?"

"*Was* a Washington intern. Note the expiration date." She tapped the plastic as he read her name.

"Ivy Dillon! I thought you looked familiar; you've grown up."

Ivy pulled out the chair and sat opposite him. The young waitress plunked down a salad bowl with a side of tuna fish for him and a plate of toast cut on the diagonal for Ivy.

"The last time we were together was on our first date."

"Yes, I remember the splendid evening," Gram nodded fondly.

"It was splendid for you. Our first date turned into our last date since you ditched me for another girl at the charity ball."

"I took you to a charity ball? Now you've lost me."

"Actually, it was a fundraiser for a community hospice but it was never built. That night the cash and checks were stolen from the safe. Of course, the checks were all cancelled but there was a huge amount of cash that disappeared."

"What a shame. There should have been another

fundraiser."

"Not around here. Once people lose their money, they lose confidence."

"That's too bad." Rob suddenly looked as though he was trying to catch a thought. "By the way, wasn't there a drowning that night?"

"Yes, there was. I still have nightmares about it."

"After all this time? I would think it would be all but forgotten by now." He eyed her a second and then turned back to his lunch.

"No, the victim was my best friend."

"I am so sorry, Ivy. I didn't mean to sound cavalier, I just didn't know."

"The dreams have different beginnings, but they all end the same with me lying at the bottom of the lake next to her body." Ivy wondered why she was even telling him this. "An outstretched skeleton hand reaching toward me."

"Creepy."

"For sure." She shivered.

"You mentioned I ditched you for someone else?"

"Erin Lowe."

"Erin Lowe," he repeated pleasantly. "She was quite a gal. Did she ever tell you what we did that night at the yacht club?"

"She didn't have to tell me. I know what happened."

"You do?"

"Don't worry! Your secret is safe with me, Congressman Gram. I know about your cover-up," Ivy cupped her right hand around her mouth.

He stared at her with wide brown eyes as all color drained from his cheeks.

"Oops, bad wording, I guess 'cover-up' isn't a phrase you want anyone to use when you're connected to politics. Let me reword that; I won't tell anyone you went down the lake to share a drink with an underage girl."

"Erin told you we *drank?*"

"No, she'd never tell, but you all came back pretty loaded. Listen, I know you're on a timeline so let me get to the point. I couldn't help but notice your security needs tightening and I wrote down a few ideas. Here." Ivy handed him her wrinkled notes. "Sorry, they're kind of messy. I can type them out for you if you'd like."

"No need to redo your notes. These will do just fine. My security people are my frat brothers from college. I guess they need some professional lessons." Gram skimmed Ivy's paper and then tucked it into the breast pocket of his suit jacket.

"I have Ms. Geneen Waters' recommendation. She's the..."

"Everyone knows who she is," he interrupted. "And you're impressive. I could use you to manage my campaign headquarters in Chicago." Rob pulled a business card from his pocket. Taking the pen from his pocket, he scribbled down information. "Here's my personal cell phone number."

"Congressman Gram, are you serious?"

"Hey, start calling me Rob. And yes, I am very serious. I like surrounding myself with old friends. Then I know I can trust them. We're like a family."

****

It was eighty-two degrees and windy in Chicago.

Ivy pushed open the heavy glass door of Congressman Gram's Congressional Re-Election headquarters. Robert waited for her in the back office.

"Welcome! This is your office. I hope it will be sufficient."

"It looks as though everything I need is right here," Ivy nodded looking around.

"Ivy, it's good to have someone keep the office organized. I'm on the road a lot and don't need the additional stresses of the operation here.” Rob took a day planner from his pocket. “I will make a copy of my schedule so you know where I’ll be on what days.”

“Hello, Ivy!” A new voice entered the conversation.

Ivy turned around to see a short, dark haired man with intense brown eyes standing in the doorway.

“Ivy, do you remember Tony Bogart?” Rob asked.

Ah, Tony Bogart; he was another chink in the chain of people from the night of the fundraiser, the same night her best friend drown. “Tony? I didn’t realize you worked for Rob, too. It’s nice to see you again.”

“Hi, yourself. You’re right, Rob, she has filled out.”

Rob turned red and chuckled uncomfortably. “Always the jokester, aren’t you, Tony?”

“A jokester who could be slapped with a lawsuit,” Ivy mused.

“Tony is my public relations person. He can get me out of any trouble with his smooth talking.” Rob boyishly poked him in the side.

“Brace yourself; it’s time to meet the staff!” Tony took Ivy by the elbow and guided her into the main room that was humming with activity and alive with ringing phones.

****

By early evening, Ivy stood at the windows of her flat, watching the truck on the street below flash its lights at children to get out of the way and then pull into the parking spot in front of her brownstone. The truck’s rear still stuck out in the street a bit which made it hard for traffic to go around. Two men got out to begin unloading the second-hand furniture from her mother’s attic. Ivy went down to the street to meet them just as her mother pulled up in her sedan. "I hope you can use everything these young men are unloading."

"I'm sure I can. See those windows on the third floor? That's my place."

"We'll have fun arranging my attic furniture!" Rita called after her daughter.

Once the movers had gone, the women moved the furniture around until they were satisfied with the placement. Rita began unpacking boxes while Ivy sat on the couch with office files spread around her.

"Why don't you stop your work for the evening? I've just popped a casserole in the oven and we can get in our nightgowns while it's heating." Rita suggested.

Ivy agreed and slid the files into her briefcase before going into the bedroom. There in the center of the dresser was a music box with porcelain figures of a man and woman dancing on the top. Still working magic, it took her breath away. It was as exquisite as she remembered. Pushing the lever, the fanciful music began slowly as the delicate movement of the golden roller hit the fragile spikes. Ivy turned it off. "Mom, please take this back home with you."

"But Sam gave it to you that Christmas when you got engaged. Now with your own place, I thought—"

"There's no room for it here."

"I don't have much room either."

"Then donate it," Ivy suggested on her way into the bathroom.

"Okay." Rita shrugged and sat down on the bed. "I suppose you never did find out the song it played?"

"No." Ivy's voice echoed from inside the bathroom as she slipped into her nightgown. Talk about Sam was always upsetting and having to listen to that damnable music box her mother kept playing was bringing her to the brink of temporary insanity.

"Do you remember what Sam said when he gave this to you? He told you that when you found out the name of the song the music box played then your world would be as it should." Rita kept playing it again and again.

"And I took it to every antique dealer and gift store in the southern lakes region to find out what the song could be." Ivy looked out the door at her mother.

"No one knew the name." Rita shook her head.

Was this an omen her life would never be right? Figures. "Mom, I've let go of the relationship and you need to let go of it, too. Speaking of letting go, have you and Daddy sold the house Sam gave me?" Ivy set the brush on the ledge of the sink and walked back out into the bedroom.

Rita turned off the music box. "We have not quite decided what to do with the house yet."

The beloved yellow house was her consolation prize for a broken engagement—a constant, painful reminder of wrecked dreams. "Just sell it. The longer it sits there the more dilapidated it gets and the value on the property decreases. It was practically a tear-down when Sam and I bought it."

"But it's such a sweet place and has good bones. I often wonder what would have happened if you and Sam had run off and gotten married without the Olivers' approval," Rita said now taking her turn in the bathroom.

"That's what Sam wanted, but I knew that it would cause an unbearable rift between him and his dad. Eventually, it would have destroyed our marriage. The only way I can find peace is by accepting Sam and I were not meant to be."

Chapter Five

Weeks later, Ivy found Rob waiting for her at the office one morning as she came in.

"I have a surprise for you, Ivy." Rob stepped aside.

A young woman in skinny jeans walked into the office. "Surprise, Ivy!"

Ivy's jaw slackened. She stared at the woman, not sure what to say, or which name to use. Jordan? Erin?

Rob soon settled that dilemma for her. "Aren't you pleased to see Erin?"

"Ah, yes, I am," Ivy answered. Wasn't Jordan in a play? Isn't Erin in hiding?

"Erin, is everything all right?"

"Fine. My play closed and Rob called to offer me the office manager job."

"Last time I looked that was my job, or am I fired?"

"Just the opposite, Ivy, I need you more than ever. The most recent polls still say the race is neck and neck. I need Erin here to do your job because I need you on the road for advice and to help write my speeches," Rob cajoled. "For instance, yesterday someone asked me how I would vote on the environment."

"How will you?" Ivy asked.

"I'm not sure which is the most politically correct way to answer. Do I address the rising gas prices, saving the spotted owls, or talk about planting a tree?"

"Yes, you do need me," she agreed, pleased with her unexpected promotion.

"Great. Since you need to show Erin what to do, I'll delay my trip to Des Plaines by a few days so you can come with me. I sure hope Erin is a fast learner because I am still in a heap of trouble with my voters in that city." Rob started to leave. "It's a make-or-break situation there for me."

"Wait," Ivy got out of her chair and stopped him at the door. "You have got to leave for Des Plaines tomorrow as planned. It could mean the difference between winning or losing the race."

"Then be ready to leave tomorrow."

"Go ahead, Ivy," Erin prodded, taking Ivy's desk chair. "How hard can it be to sit here and tell everyone out there to pipe down and get busy?"

"It's not that simple," Ivy said looking around. "All right, I'll go with you, Rob. Let me work late tonight so I can leave with you in the morning."

"Good choice, Ivy!" Erin cheered. "I think I'll mingle with the staff right now. I see some cute men out there." Erin winked at Rob before walking out.

Rob lingered. "One more thing, Ivy. Erin needs a place to live. I told her she can move in with you. I know this is short notice..."

"No problem."

"Okay, I'm on my way out, but if you're still here after dark, be sure the front door is locked."

****

Ivy made a bedroom for Erin out of the walk-in pantry.

She pulled out the cot and laid out fresh sheets while trying to grasp the new situation. "I thought you hated politics and here you are working for a campaign."

"Have you forgotten that I once was the editor for an underground paper during college? I am returning to my first love."

"How did you hear about this job? I knew nothing about it until you showed up."

"I came to Chicago for an audition and ran into Rob. Imagine my surprise when he told me you were working for him. Here we are roomies again. Gossip time. Tell me about Rob and Tony," Erin asked, tucking the sheet under the thin mattress.

"What's to say? They are handsome, wealthy and important."

"It looks like things have pretty much stayed the same for them."

"Yeah, but they are *more* handsome, *more* wealthy, and *more* important." Ivy laughed.

Erin took out an old photo of three teenage girls posing arm in arm on a pier; Erin, Ivy and Karin. She handed it to Ivy who smiled and rubbed her hand over the glass before setting the framed picture on the shelf.

"There's something I've wanted to ask you and never had the nerve."

"What?" Erin gave Ivy her full attention.

"Do you ever have dreams about Karin?"

Erin sat on the cot and made room for Ivy. "No. The past is done."

"I can't seem to accept it the way you have. I often dream about the night Karin was murdered."

"Murdered?" Erin furrowed her brows. "My parents told me it was an accidental drowning."

"Yes, that's what the authorities said, too, but I think Karin was murdered."

"That's plain crazy!" Erin rubbed her arms.

"Think about it. Karin never would have gone down to the lake alone."

"Lots of kids went swimming that night. Karin went along with them."

"But she wasn't found near the Yacht Club where everyone swam, but way down the lake, near Lake Katherine on the Illinois side. I'm the one who found her body, remember?"

"I do remember, but you found her a few houses down from the club."

"No, it was miles and someday, I'll find out what really happened." Ivy looked at the clock. "If I'm going with Rob tomorrow, I better get back to the office. You might want to meet me back at the office later so I can show you what needs to be done."

****

It was late in the evening and Ivy was finishing up the schedules when she heard a noise from the front room. The office keys were on her desk in front of her and she realized she hadn't taken the time to lock the door.

"Ivy, are you still here?" Erin stepped into the light of her doorway.

The sudden release of fear shot adrenalin through Ivy making her wheeze. She dove for her purse and dug for the inhaler. Finding it, she blasted her lungs.

"I didn't mean to frighten you. Sorry about that but you did tell me to come back tonight."

"That's all right, I had forgotten." Ivy tossed the keys to Erin. "Go lock up."

When Erin returned, she pulled up a chair next to Ivy.

"By the way, what's the latest on the 'Voice'? Any more calls?" Ivy asked.

"Not one since you left Washington."

"Since I left? But he always asked for you. How strange." Ivy couldn't figure how the 'Voice' just dropped out of their lives after being such a scary presence for so long. With a long night ahead of them, she shrugged it off for now. Whatzhisname was probably right about it being an old boyfriend. "Here's a list of employee names and what they do. I have the schedules made out for the next several weeks. I keep them in a file in my left drawer and try to post them a week in advance. You will also be handling the petty cash." Ivy opened the logbook and the last page caught her attention. "Erin, look at this entry…does it seem strange to you? The two figures do not add up."

Erin shook her head. "I'm not sure what I'm seeing."

"Let me explain. A thousand dollars was taken out for petty cash today and the items listed do not cost that much. See? Lunch for five people at a sandwich place plus taxi fare."

"Wow, someone's a big tipper!" Erin whistled.

"Everyone who works here knows the system for expenditures. For anything over a hundred dollars, it has to be first 'okayed' by me and then by one other of the salaried personnel. But this one wasn't, I wonder why."

"Maybe you weren't here for them to get your signature," Erin supposed. "You helped me get settled in your place, remember?"

"I was here at that time. We didn't leave until late afternoon and this took place earlier in the day. Receipts must accompany all purchases for validation and there aren't any here."

Erin slid across the desk and picked up the logbook to look at it one more time. She paged through it. "Hey, look, there are other entries that are similar but way back here in the book. The dates start from the beginning of the campaign." Erin searched for amounts over a hundred dollars. She wrote them down and then added them up.

"This is the first I've seen this. Why are they put at the back of the logbook and not in sequence by dates?" Ivy looked closely at the signatures. Each one resembled Tony's handwriting but some of the names were Robert Gram. The more recent entries had her name. *Forgery*. "He's using these funds as if it they are his own and putting us on the hook for his spending."

"Are you going to turn him in?" Erin asked excitedly.

"Tempting isn't it? We could all go to jail for this. First, I'm telling Rob." Ivy slid the paper into the logbook and then put both into a large brown envelope to take home for safekeeping. "It's time to have a serious talk with Rob in the morning."

****

"Ivy, Ivy! Wake up!"

Ivy lunged forward in bed wheezing. "My inhaler," she eked.

Erin searched the bedroom. "I can't find your inhaler anywhere!"

"Purse." Ivy pointed toward the living room. In a moment, she heard her purse's contents being dumped out and Erin raking through it. "Ivy, it's not here!"

"Paper bag…kitchen…" she eked.

Seconds later, Erin ran back into the bedroom, shaking open a brown paper bag. With her last shot of strength, Ivy covered her nose and mouth with the bag. She exhaled, inhaled, exhaled, creating loud crinkling noises. "Thanks…it worked…I can breath."

"I don't think you should go with Rob today. Stay home and rest. I've never seen you have such a bad attack."

"I'll be fine." Ivy got out of bed and looked in the bathroom cabinet for her inhaler. "I need…call the pharmacy…to pick up another…"

"I'll make that call for you." Erin went for the phone.

"There are three refills left…before I see the doctor." She patted her chest.

"Okay, I'm calling right now."

Ivy was packed and ready for Rob by the time his security came to the door to carry her suitcases down to the awaiting limousine. Ivy followed and slid into the backseat next to Rob.

He frowned. “Good morning, you look rather tired this morning; are you all right?”

“We need to talk. There’s something you should know.” Ivy reached into her briefcase for the logbook encased in the brown envelope. The window dividing the driver from the passengers slid open and there was Tony Bogart. “Good morning, Ivy!”

“Tony, I didn’t expect to see you…” Ivy froze.

“I bet you didn’t,” he answered, slowly accompanied by an ear-to-ear smile.

“What did you want to show me?” Rob nudged Ivy.

“Never mind. It can keep until later.” She tucked the mailer back into her briefcase. “Before we get out of the city, I need to stop at the drugstore on the corner of Wellington and Clark Street. I misplaced my inhaler.”

Tony held up an inhaler with her name on it. Her face turned bright red when she suddenly remembered she had left the container at the office, perched at the edge of her desk.

“Feels like there’s enough to keep ya breathing until we’re back in town.” Tony winked.

****

Nightfall.

Ivy was tired of standing all day in hose and heels. Tonight was all about bare feet, baggy jeans and honesty. The brown mailer was open on the table and the logbook neatly bookmarked in all the right places. The logbook was in Rob’s hands. He looked devastated over his friend’s betrayal and sat shaking his head.

“Contributors and tax attorneys don’t like this, I promise! If this should get out to the press, heaven help us all. Who wins this election will be the least of your concerns.”

“This has got to be wrong. Tony wouldn’t do this

to me." Rob began to perspire.

"Rob, it's here in black and white, with his signature on some and then forgery on the others." Ivy pointed.

"You'd think he'd be a better con man than this, huh?" Rob chuckled.

"What are you saying? That you wished he had done a better job at his deception? Rob, what will you do when the books are gone over? Never mind about your political aspirations, this means jail time."

Rob held up his hand. "I'll take care of this in my own way. I don't see how I can fire him at this point in the campaign, but I can make it so the funds are replaced and any future amounts are not available to him."

"You have got to fire Tony," Ivy insisted. "And turn over these books."

The door to the room banged shut so hard that it made Ivy jump. "Was someone just eavesdropping?"

"I'll check." He opened the door and returned a few minutes later. "Whoever it was is gone now. Back to what we were saying…"

"You should contact the FBI before someone turns you in." She studied his face for some hint of honesty.

"Are you threatening me?" He raised his eyebrows.

"Rob, of course not—no."

"The race is too close. I am leading my opponent by less than five percentage points. This will sink me for sure." He dumped the book onto the tabletop. "Today was a great day. We'll build on that. In the meantime, I'll take the book with me. Just keep quiet about our discussion tonight and you'll have a long political career. If not, I can guarantee you a cashier job back home right next to Lucy."

Ivy shot him a nasty look and walked out of his

suite, leaving him sitting there with the information in his hand. Thinking that might have been a dumb move on her part, she considered returning for the documents as she crossed the carpeted hallway and pushed the button for the elevator to take her to her floor. Waiting for it to arrive, Ivy couldn't help but be confused about Rob's decision. It made her ashamed to be associated with him. As soon as she stepped out on her floor, Ivy had a feeling of being watched and sprinted to the door. Inside the room, the eerie feeling continued. Without hesitation, she turned on the light and remained in the doorway looking around. Slowly, she pushed open the bathroom door until it hit against the wall. Ivy shoved the shower curtain to one side. "This room is clear," she whispered hopefully. Back in the bedroom, she checked her belongings. Nothing was missing. Still she couldn't shake the thought it had been touched, gone over, looked at, and held. On impulse, she slid to her knees and peeked under the bed. "Clear here, too." Ivy sighed and got to her feet.

Too tired for a shower, she changed into her nightgown and slipped into bed. As she stretched out, her foot brushed against something spiky. Stifling a scream, she bolted up and yanked off the covers to see a bony hand, void of flesh, with skeletal fingers reaching upward toward the direction of her face. It made her dive for the phone. In seconds, Rob was on the line. A few minutes later, security was in her room.

Rob did his best to console Ivy as she frantically wept and threw her clothes into her suitcase. "I'm leaving! Tonight! Someone on your team is trying to frighten me and they have done a good job of it!"

"I want the security tapes of the floor," Rob hollered to the hotel security.

"Management is going over them now, sir."

"I want them!" Rob insisted loudly.

Ivy reeled around. "Why? So you can add that to the stack of things you aren't sharing with the police?"

Rob took a hold of Ivy's arm and walked her into the bathroom. He slammed the door and turned on the water full blast. "Don't you ever say anything like that again out in public; do you hear me?" he seethed.

"You don't care much for witnesses, do you?" she spat right back.

"I'm barely hanging in the lead. One innuendo hits the paper and I'm done!"

"Since you are not going to do anything about any of this, I'm handing in my resignation the minute I get back to the city."

Rob paled and his voice softened. "Please, don't do that. Stay on board at least until the end of the election and then if you still want to leave, I'll not only write you a glowing recommendation but I'll make phone calls. Ivy, I really can't win this without you."

Ivy hesitated.

"Please."

"Okay, against my better judgment, I'll stay."

"One more thing, don't say anything to anyone about tonight."

Ivy pushed him to the side and walked out of the bathroom where a security guard waited.

"Ma'am, this skeleton hand isn't real. It's plastic. I think someone is just fun'n you. This is nothing more than a gag gift people use at Halloween."

Chapter Six

First Erin shows up unexpectedly.

Next Rob threatens her.

If things come in threes, then Ivy wasn't at all surprised when a call from the DC police came. "I think we may have recovered some of your items from a robbery just over a year ago. We need you to identify your belongings."

"Nearly everything has been replaced. Can't I just skip going? After all I live in Chicago now and this isn't a good time for me to be gone," she tried to explain.

"We need all the victims to come in to identify their belongings in order to have a strong case. You don't want these criminals to go free, do you?"

"What items of mine have been recovered?" Even if it had been her laptop, she was sure it would be in bad shape by now; outdated at the least.

"I can't say what has been recovered. Only you can do that by personally coming." The officer was clearly agitated.

"All right. I'll fly to Washington with my roommate, who also lived with me at the time," Ivy promised before hanging up.

Erin and Ivy flew standby. It was a picture perfect landing under blue skies and it felt good to be back in DC again as they rode the bus into the city. Ivy watched out the window as Erin watched the cute guy across the aisle from them.

"Look, there is the Washington Monument which reminds me, I want to call Ms. Waters to invite her to lunch." Ivy pressed her numbers and listened to her private line ring until the voicemail picked up. "Ms. Waters, this is Ivy Dillon. I'm in Washington for just today and would love to see you before I leave. Can we meet for lunch? Call me back."

At police headquarters, Ivy and Erin were led to a room filled with treasures. Dozens of eight-foot long tables displayed the stolen goods. Each item had been assigned a number. There were jewels, silver, and enough electronics to start a warehouse.

"This is like a giant estate sale," Ivy said.

"Only you're not allowed to buy anything. Bummer," Erin complained.

"This isn't a shopping spree, ladies. Do you see anything of yours that I can tag with your initials?" the officer sourly asked.

They located some of their items. Ivy couldn't help noticing how insignificant her small radio and bargain TV were. It wasn't surprising that her laptop wasn't in the mix, but what did surprise her was finding some of her old books that she didn't even realize had been taken. Ivy opened the covers and inside they all had her name neatly printed. Someone's nasty fingers and hands had been all over everything. Neither Erin nor she wanted any of it back, not ever. Now that they had performed their civic duty, it was time for lunch.

They picked their favorite restaurant on H Street. Ivy tried another call to Ms. Waters but got her voicemail.

As they returned to the airport, Ivy lamented not being able to see her old mentor. Their flight back to Chicago was uneventful and by the time, the plane's wheels touched down at O'Hare, they hadn't even been gone twelve hours.

****

Ivy lay restless in bed, staring up at the ceiling,

thinking over the last few days. Rob's threatening words tumbled around in her head. His terms had been punctuated with the strategic placement of the skeleton hand. No matter how many times he denied it, she knew he had it planted there. Rob was adept at learning people's weaknesses and then using it against them. She had been stupid to open up her mouth about her nightmare in the first place and now he was using her fears to control her. She wondered how she could continue working for a despicable man without ethics. Maybe she had a skeleton hand in her dreams but Rob had a closet filled with skeletons. Ivy decided to pick some of those bones to hold over Rob's head. It'd be her bargaining tool.

Since sleep wasn't happening anytime soon, she took a gamble and went to the office to check on things and begin her list of memos. There were a myriad of tasks to be completed and Ivy wrote her list in her day planner so she wouldn't forget what needed to be done and could cross things off as she accomplished them.

She unlocked the door and then dove to disarm the alarm. It only had a thirty second delay. After rearming it, Ivy turned off the overhead light and in the darkness began to slowly move toward her private office. Just feet away from her door, she turned to have a look at Tony's desk in a little alcove all by itself. The outside light coming in through the window illuminated the desk. She closed the blinds and, on a hunch, she jerked on the drawers but none of them budged, all locked up tight. If she wanted in, she'd have to break the lock.

Ivy sat on the chair in front of the computer and turned it on. The blue screen light flickered as the computer loaded. Once the system was up, Ivy tried to get into the documents but they were protected by a password. Since she didn't know his password, she shut down the system to find another way around his locks. Ivy chuckled to herself as she came up with a plan. Rushing to the supply cabinet, she grabbed a hard drive that she had removed from a computer they no longer had. Since she had done the computer updates, she knew the systems were all compatible and it would take Tony some time to figure out what had happened.

Back at Tony's desk, Ivy quickly opened the door in the rear of the computer and slid out the hard drive currently installed, replacing it with the new one. After checking his desk to make sure that everything looked to be back in its place, she grabbed her purse. She emptied out her make-up case and put the hard drive in it so it wouldn't be noticeable to anyone who casually glanced into her purse.

Pleased with herself, Ivy headed toward her office. There was a noise. Ivy held her purse tightly and hurried into her office where she closed the door behind her. Several minutes passed. It remained quiet but just to be sure, she peeked back out, hoping there wouldn't be a stranger or an enemy floating toward her from the darkness.

"Hello? Anyone there?" There was only a room filled with silhouettes of furniture. Ivy slammed the door and ran behind her desk. Perhaps she should look for a weapon, just in case. In the top drawer, she found a letter opener and placed it on top of the desk. For another moment, there was only the sound of her breath. Then just as she got to work, there was a thud followed by distinct footsteps. Ivy reached for the letter opener and held on to it as a dagger.

She left her office and tried to make her way through the maze of desks and chairs, feeling along the wall, moving toward the light switch at the front. Reaching it, she flipped it on. The overhead iridescent lights momentarily blinded her. The palms of her hand were sweaty but she kept a tight grip on the weapon. Just as her eyes adjusted to the light, there was another sound. Now it came from the back of the room. Ivy moved in that direction. There was a sharp curve to the wall and she felt certain someone was just on the other side of it. As she rounded the corner, arms went around her. She screamed.

"Lower your voice, will you, Ivy!" the man yelled, obviously as startled as she was.

"Tony! What are you doing here?" Ivy felt her pulse in her throat.

"I am just getting a few things." He brushed passed her and went to his desk; taking a key from his pocket and fitting it into the small metal lock. With a click, the drawer opened and he took out some papers, folded them over once and shoved them into the inside of his jacket.

Ivy kept looking at his computer, praying he would not push the button to turn it on. Not now. He was supposed to do that when it was broad daylight and there were many other suspects in the room. Not in the dead of night with only her to blame.

"How did you get in here? I locked the door and set the alarm."

"I'm in charge of security, remember?" Tony shoved her sideways into the wall as he staggered away.

She rubbed her aching shoulder, "Tony, you've been drinking."

"Want to join me for another? There's a little bar just around the corner that may still be open. Come on and go with me. I am sure we can work our differences out."

Ivy walked to the closest desk with a phone. Tony grabbed her hard making her drop the letter opener.

The last thing she wanted to do was make him angrier. Masking her fear she sweetly said, "Tony, go home. I'll call you a cab."

"I am trying very hard to get along with you but you are making things impossible for me. Your little plan to discredit me didn't work because I know about all the secrets and you don't know any, not one. Those secrets make me more powerful than Rob."

"And just what secrets are those?" Ivy did her best to compose herself. She reached down trying to locate the weapon, keeping her eyes trained on him. Tony kicked the opener out of the way with the toe of his shoe. The opener disappeared behind a metal cabinet.

"Just secrets." His smile was thin, his eyes filled with hatred. Then he came at her.

She ran for the back office. Halfway there, Tony tackled her. Ivy hit the floor hard, knocking the wind out of her.

Ivy twisted around and kicked at his legs. She used her fingernails as claws and tried to scratch him but it was no use. She couldn't reach his face and he wore long sleeves. Tony yanked her up by the root of the hair. Then once they got into the office, he backhanded her. Ivy flew against the metal cabinet. Tony staggered out the front door, leaving it wide open.

For several minutes, Ivy couldn't move. When she was certain Tony had really gone, she crawled to the desk where she pulled herself up on legs that refused to hold her weight. Ivy fell back into the chair. It was important for her to get to the front door and get it locked behind Tony or anyone walking down the street might take a fancy to walk through an open door in the dead of night.

Finally, on her feet, Ivy limped toward the front. The street door was banging against the wall in the wind. The night breeze felt good coiling around her, clearing her mind. It took all her remaining strength to push the door shut. She snapped one lock and then hurried back to her office for the phone. It was then she noticed the blood on her hands. On the wall hung a mirror where she saw her reflection. Her face was red and swollen. Two bruising eyes stared blankly back at her. Her left cheekbone was purple and her forehead above one eye was black with a deep cut sliced into it. Blood ran out.

Again Ivy reached for the phone. She would tell the police, not only about Tony beating her, but also about the logbook. He'd be sorry. She'd get him. He'd be arrested and thrown into jail. Since Rob wouldn't do anything about Tony, then she would.

Pushing nine and then one before pausing, she stopped and set the phone down. A terrible scenario played out in her head. Rob would sacrifice her to protect Tony. She knew that as clearly as she knew her own name.

No longer could she be a part of this campaign, and in that moment, she decided to resign. Tonight. It was dangerous to stick around. She had to get out of the city. Somewhere safe where she could decide what her next move would be. Ivy thought about the cabins in Door County where her family vacationed when she was little. Suddenly, the path seemed so clear to her.

Ivy typed out her resignation and then emailed it to Rob and all the employees. She headed home to pack her clothes and rent a car. With a bit of the Lord's protection, she'd hide from Tony. It wouldn't take him long to figure she had his hard drive and he'd surely come for it. She strongly suspected the money he stole was only the tip of the iceberg. If she was right, whatever was on the hard drive would put her into jeopardy.

Chapter Seven

A month later, Ivy's bruises had healed and she had had enough of hiding out, leaving the north woods cabin. The plan was to collect the rest of her belongings in Chicago, sublease her apartment to Erin, and return home to Twin Lakes for a season until she figured out her life. Working beside Lucy at the Café seemed a preferable occupation to what she had just been through.

And if God were in the prayer answering business, Whatzhisname would walk in, sit at the counter and ask her to pour him a cup of coffee. Maybe she could persuade him to stay in town for awhile, or maybe for the rest of his life. It made her wonder what he did for a living and if it had anything to do with why he left so quickly. The thought suddenly occurred to her that perhaps he was on the run from the police and when her apartment was robbed he figured he needed to immediately move away. Perhaps he was the culprit. Ivy laughed at herself and waved away her silly thoughts.

It was good to be near home again. Chicago was still miles away and she added to the distance by taking the scenic route. The tires rolled over familiar country roads as Ivy put down the car windows and enjoyed the lovely breeze.

A dark sedan cruised up from behind and crowded her bumper. It was difficult to concentrate with it so close. The car seemed to get closer as she drove and was making her more nervous. At the next corner, Ivy felt the need to get as far as she could away from it and took the next left onto a gravel road, glad to see the car speed up and disappear down the road.

The narrow gravel lane was hemmed in tightly on both sides with woods. Mosquitoes were fierce so she rolled up the windows tight. Five deep ruts later she reached a dead end. Carefully, she backed the car around not wanting to end up in the ditch, and then headed back in the direction she came.

On County O again, it was disconcerting when that same vehicle was back in her rearview mirror. The driver tooted the horn. Ivy signaled for him to go around but it stayed put, still inches from her back bumper. Minutes later, she caught a sudden movement out of the corner of her eye as the vehicle pulled up alongside and the driver pointed for her to pull off the road, near an orchard of apple trees. It was a fairly isolated location. Panic spiked when she saw the double yellow line in the road and a hill fast approaching. Accelerating would do no good on these gouged roads, for everyone would end up wound about a hefty tree. Ivy focused her eyes on the top of the hill. Again he honked at her and then it dropped behind, tailgating for miles.

At the last minute, Ivy made a quick turn to the right hoping the car would glide right on by. It did. Her sigh of relief didn't last long when, for the second time, it pulled up next to her with the window rolled down. The driver shouted at her, demanding she pull over. Now he went for something inside his pocket. Expecting to see a gun, Ivy pressed the gas pedal. The car hit eighty miles an hour and careened down the patchy road.

A tractor hauling hay, lazily pulled out in front of her. Ivy slammed on her brakes hard, which sent her chest into the steering wheel despite her seat belt. The tires squealed. Thankfully, she was still on the road and not engine deep in a ditch. Ivy's heart thumped wildly in her chest as beads of sweat formed a single line along her brow. Nervously glancing in the rearview mirror, she saw the other vehicle was now nearly one with her bumper.

"God, I'd appreciate you getting these crazies off my tail!"

Pausing at a four-way stop, the tractor turned left and Ivy decided to turn right. If she could get off the remote roads, she might have a chance to flag someone down for help. Without warning, the other car rocketed out from behind. Spinning about, it met her engine to engine. This was a maneuver she hadn't counted on. Ivy shoved her car into reverse but before she could turn it fully back around, four men popped out. In seconds men dressed in basic black were all over her vehicle. "Open up!" One of them ordered.

"No!"

One of them smashed her back window with a baton. Flying glass whipped about her as Ivy screamed at them. "Hey, take it easy! This is a rental!"

Wrenched by her elbow from the car, she immediately was shoved into the backseat of their vehicle, facing two men. One resembled a cement block. The second man had angular features, green eyes, and a feel-good smile—Whatzhisname.

"It's you!" Ivy gasped and her hands flew over her chest.

"And so we meet again."

"What is this all about?!" She shook uncontrollably.

"We're with the FBI. Forgive us for interrupting your day," Whatzhisname gently spoke, threading his fingers through his graying hair that still curled up along the collar.

"Hey, can I have my purse? My inhaler…is

inside...and I'm feeling my...throat tighten. I have trouble...breath...ing during times of...stress...I think...this...qualifies," she huffed, feeling faint.

Whatzhisname moved to her right and poked through her bag. He handed her the inhaler. She used it, closed her eyes and leaned her head back.

"There is a matter of national security to discuss with you."

"You want to discuss national security with *me*? Who are you really?" Ivy crossed one arm over the other.

"Do you know Ms. Geneen Waters?"

"Of course, I was her intern," Ivy proudly stated. "You had me so scared for a minute! Now I know what this is about."

"We thought you might," the cement block said.

"She sent you to pick up my intern badge. I'm so sorry I forgot to hand it in when I left. This breach of security is a terrible offense but it was an honest oversight, really. Don't worry, I'll get it back to you as soon as possible. That's a promise. I just have to find what I did with it. It used to be in my purse, but now, I think it's home in one of my dresser drawers. Next time phone me, it's much less threatening. Now where's my car? I have to have it back before five or I'll be charged with an extra day rental."

"I'm not here about your badge." Whatzhisname smiled.

"Then what is this about?"

"Don't you watch the news?" the cement block asked.

"Of course I do! But these past weeks I've been out of touch...resting."

"Ivy, we have some bad news for you. Show her, please, Agent Molinar."

Now she knew the name of the cement block.

Molinar unfolded a newspaper and passed it to her. The headlines read: PREZ SECRETARY DEAD

AT AGE SIXTY-FOUR. "She was found on the riverbank of the Potomac."

Ivy sat motionless as she read the headlines over and over. She shut her eyes tight as tears squeezed out. Finally, Ivy's eyes flew open. "It's impossible! She belonged to the President; I mean she worked right by his office door and she was nice! The President wouldn't let anything happen to her."

They motored down a grassy path hemmed in on either side with trees as branches scratched along both sides of the car. The driver stopped when they were deep in green shadows. Paranoia mixed with claustrophobia gave Ivy an underwater feeling and her ears began to ring. How she wanted to reach the top of the water where there was air and sky and birds. She was sinking quickly. "Oh God, help me! I gotta get out of this car…now!"

The men sat stone-faced. Not moving.

"Fair warning…I'm about to get sick."

Three doors popped opened as the agents leaped out. Ivy slowly exited, one foot on the dirt road, then the other. So this is where her life ended. Her pitiable parents would hear about it on the five o'clock news either today or first thing tomorrow. No that's wrong; the police would come to the door to tell them first, then they'd hear it on the news.

"Before you kill me, I have one request…what is this about anyway?" Ivy coughed. "I don't want to go to my…grave…wondering. It would also be a good thing to know in case I'm not the one you're really after. This might be a good time to discover it." Strange, her throat suddenly opened. Ah, fresh air.

Whatzhisname laughed raucously. "Dear Ivy, we didn't mean to frighten you although I see we have already done a good job of it. We should have introduced ourselves to you all ready. Forgive us the oversight; sometimes we tend to be overzealous. I'm Senior Special Agent Ian Serby, the driver is Special

Agent Roebuck, and this is Rookie Agent Molinar. The man driving your rental is my partner, FBI Detective Mitchell. We're not here to execute you. We're here to help you." His posture was military straight.

In unison, all three men flipped open their credentials. One by one, Ivy carefully looked at them. They did appear to be official but she still wasn't sure. "You've been following me for quite a while." Ivy pointed at Serby. "Why?"

"It's part of the case that I cannot discuss."

It made no sense but for some reason at that moment she gave him her trust. Maybe it was because in this isolated area she needed someone to trust. "If Ms. Waters has been missing for months, how come it isn't all over the news?"

"The President and her family agreed to keep it quiet as we investigated. We would like to question you at the FBI Headquarters."

"I can't see why; I don't know anything that'll be of help to you. So, why don't you just let me go my way?"

"It's unsafe for you to be driving it in its condition," Serby told her.

"And whose fault is that, Agent Serby?" Ivy glared.

"Call me, Ian. I will personally have the window repaired and return it to the rental company."

"Then how will I get back?" Ivy looked around at the wilderness.

"With me, of course." Ian smiled.

The rental vehicle appeared from around the trees and came to a full stop, feet away from her. One of the agents popped the trunk, got her belongings and deposited them in to their trunk. And just like that, they were back on the road.

"I have some pictures I want you to look at. Tell me if you recognize any of these faces." Ian passed

Ivy a folder.

Ivy looked from face to face. One was a mug shot. “Yes, I have seen these men.”

“Where?” Ian asked.

“They’re on Congressman Gram’s private security team.”

Chapter Eight

Seven days had passed and Ivy found herself replaying her conversation with Ian. It was disconcerting to realize she had actually worked for such a low life as Rob. If anything, she learned her lesson. From now on she'd interview her perspective employers as much as they interviewed her. Maybe even more.

If she had her druthers, she'd never have returned to the city but would have gone directly home. Loose ends needed to be tied up such as a change of address with the post office and transferring the utility bills to her roommate's name. It was also important to have only Erin's name on the lease in case she suddenly blew back out of town. The truth of the matter was Ivy also needed the rest of her belongings. However, with every noise from the street, or in the hallway, she'd freeze in place wondering if it were Rob coming for her or Ian. She rubbed her temples trying to wipe away her romantic thoughts of Ian but then he'd show up that night in her dreams, keeping her safe, watching over her.

Now she was finally back home. Parked in front of her little house on the inlet. Ivy removed her belongings from the car and slammed the trunk. She struggled up the steps to her parent's front door with all her suitcases in tow and Ian in her heart.

Ivy closed the door behind her and facing the kitchen, she set her things down in the hall. "I'm home!" she called out rounding the corner. There in the living room, balancing flea market teacups on their knees were three FBI men in dark suits—Senior FBI Agent Ian Serby was there. The sight of him was enough to buckle her knees. Ivy gripped the edge of the table while doing her best to hide her happiness. He had come on business. "Ian!" She knew her face and the tenor of her voice gave her excitement away.

A smile spread over Ian's face as he stood and walked to her. "Ivy, it's good to see you've arrived safely. We've been worried about you."

It was only then she noticed his partners, Agent Josh Roebuck and Rookie Agent Frisco Molinar.

"My 'men in black' are back." Ivy quickly covered, pretending to be displeased. She bit back her next smile hoping no one could read her thoughts. "I just hope they didn't smash any windows on their way into the house."

"What?" her mother asked. "Ivy, these men say they are from the FBI and showed us their credentials." Rita worried.

"For some reason they think I hold a key to national security." Ivy sat in the chair.

"Actually," there was an awkward silence before Ian spoke, "Ivy Dillon, we're here to take you into custody."

"Custody?" her father echoed in surprise.

"Mr. Dillon," Agent Molinar stepped in. "Your daughter is an important witness in an ongoing investigation of national interest. If she doesn't come willingly, then we will have to arrest her."

"Oh, my," her mother began to shed tears. "Don't let anyone hurt her."

"Mom, it's really all right, don't cry." Ivy turned inquisitive when speaking to the agents, "What's changed in the last week?"

"Quite a bit but we are not in a secure location to discuss it. Please, every moment is critical. We need to leave." Ian seemed jittery.

"Okay but I just now walked in from Chicago. I need to take my suitcases to my room and repack." Ivy headed up the stairs wondering if she should climb out the window.

In her bedroom, Ivy could hardly put her thoughts together. She opened her bureau drawers and exchanged the clothes from her suitcase. Casual jeans and shirts seemed right, although she questioned how many to take.

"They can't keep me too long." Ivy reassured herself that this would be a quick trip with few clothes needed. She slid Tony's hard drive between her clothes and then, as an afterthought, packed the book on Ancient Egypt and her Bible from her side table drawer.

Ivy didn't hear her mom come into the room. "Can I help you get ready?"

"I'm way ahead of you, Mom." Ivy pointed at her Bible and then snapped closed her suitcase.

Rita stepped closer and whispered, "That's not what I meant. Here…" She opened Ivy's hand and placed a thick wad of money in it along with a cashier's check made out to cash. It was for many thousands of dollars.

"Mom? Where'd you get this?" Ivy gasped.

She turned toward the door and closed it tight. "I did as you asked. The yellow house is sold."

"Wow, you drag your feet for years and then overnight it's sold."

"Not overnight. As you said, it's been years but I recently sold it to the county."

"Not the county! All they do is tear things down to put up strip malls or pour cement over dreams to make way for a highway." Ivy felt sick to her stomach.

"What?"

"Never mind." Ivy handed the cash and check

back to her mother.

"It seems I did something wrong again," her mom said with a sigh.

"No, it's all right. I'm glad you sold the house. It was falling to pieces just sitting there. I think you and Dad ought to keep the money though."

Her mother gently placed a hand on Ivy's arm. "Honey, this is your money and I have a feeling you are going to need it."

Taking the money, Ivy hugged her mother tightly and noticed she felt thinner than usual. "Mom, are you feeling all right?"

"Of course dear..." Her mother squeezed tightly one more time and then stepped away.

Ivy shoved the money down in her jeans pocket, the old pants from college with the hidden pocket. Then she picked up her single suitcase and padded down the steps and into the living room.

"I guess I'm ready." Ivy set the suitcase down.

Her dad got up from the chair and crossed the room to give her a hug. "Here I thought we'd have you home for a little while. Never imagined you'd turn right around and walk back out the same door you came through an hour earlier."

Ivy's eyes moistened. "Me either, Dad. As soon as I can, I'll be home again."

"I'll make your favorite dinner of macaroni and cheese with hot dogs. It'll be the first meal on the menu."

"I can't wait for that meal, Dad." Then Ivy hugged her mother. "I love you, Mom; pray for me?"

"I've never stopped."

Ivy grabbed the handle on her suitcase. Mustering up every ounce of courage, she said, "I am ready now, Agent Serby."

****

They drove away in the pitch of night.

"Agent, I don't like that you came to my parent's

house and took me into protective custody right in front of them. It couldn't have been easy for them to see me drive off in the dead of night with you. You need to solve this murder fast. I'm sure Ms. Waters' family needs closure as well," Ivy scolded.

"You know what I like about you? You've got attitude. That feistiness will take you a long way," Ian said with a laugh. Then he got out a pad of paper and pen for notes. "Okay, we'll get right to work then, since we need to move along. Let's start by focusing on the conversation you and Ms. Waters overheard."

"What are you talking about?"

Ian moved uneasily. "You two were in a west wing hallway. You were delivering booklets and stumbled, dropping the papers…"

"Oh yes, that's right. Forgive me, it's been a while." Ivy rubbed her head trying to bring back the full memory. In a few minutes, she spoke, "There was mention that something was missing. It was lost or mislaid."

"Very good." Ian wrote his notes using a penlight. "What else?"

Ivy twisted up her face searching her memory, trying to recall that day, the conversation. It was hard to remember. *Lord, help me clear my mind.* "The second man said their boss was going to be really mad about it. Their plans were ruined because this..." Ivy searched for the correct word, "thingie that was essential to their plan was now gone."

"Did the 'thingie' have a name?" Ian didn't look too pleased at her word choice.

"Yes, it was a technical word but I can't recall, sorry."

"How about the words mainframe or prototype?"

"Yes! Those exact words were used," Ivy declared.

"Good, very good." He wrote some more. "Did

you hear names or see faces?"

"No names were mentioned, that I'm very sure about. I listened for a name to be dropped so I would know who was involved but they never used one. As for faces, I didn't see them." Ivy looked at Ian and then beyond, through the window behind him, out into the pitch of night. "The same day I heard the conversation, my apartment was burgled and that's when I found you in the apartment above me. Maybe you're the one who robbed us?"

"Non, pas alores."

"Ah, so you speak French, too?" Ivy rose up.

"Un peu. I had nothing to do with the burglary but I am glad I could help you that night. I can't be sure but I feel it had something to do with finding the missing…thingie, I believe was the technical terminology you used." Ian seemed highly amused.

"My apartment is the last place it would have been. I don't see the connection."

"Perhaps later you will."

"If indeed that is the case, they wasted their time. Look, I need a straight, honest answer about something. I don't like people who lie to me."

Ian agreed. "I don't like being double-crossed myself so I will be honest with you." He spoke as though he had experience with each. "It's taken a lot of faith and courage for you to come with us tonight."

"You mean I had a choice? I don't think so. How long have you followed me and for what purpose?"

"What makes you think I was following *you*?"

"The first time I saw you was at the cast party and then you turn up as a tenant in my building. Next, you turn up in a small town café, then on the country road, and now my home. Kinda has the earmarks of being followed," Ivy spoke sarcastically.

"I will address each supposition. I was at the party with someone else when you, my dear, developed an instant crush on me…"

"I beg your pardon!" Ivy guffawed.

"It's true...hear me out." He smiled, obviously sure of himself. "And because of your stalkerish behavior—"

"Stalkerish behavior?" Ivy reeled with anger.

"I had to leave the party early just to get away from you. Secondly, I lived in *my* apartment for months before you even knew I lived there."

"What was the big hurry to leave?"

"I believe you asked me the night you brought dinner, if I was moving in or out. I was in the process of moving out. The process was completed by early the next morning."

"You forgot to check on me," she reminded him softly with a lift of her brow.

"And as for the café, I was following someone—not you—that day when you came barging into the establishment. You nearly blew my cover and I had no choice but to leave."

"If I wasn't the object of your behavior, who?"

"That I cannot disclose at this time."

Ian seemed a tad arrogant and deceptive to Ivy. "I'm beginning to think FBI stands for **F**ooled **B**y **I**an. Where are we really going tonight?"

"I told you, FBI headquarters in Chicago. We have a room there for you to stay while you are debriefed, then we'll assign you a new name and new location to live until the trial."

"A new name and location? And when is the trial?" Ivy had to know.

"After we have enough evidence," he told her.

She hiccupped.

He smiled slightly and looked down at his notes.

"Since Geneen Waters' death, I'm all you have, aren't I?"

"You'll be enough."

"I'm it? I'm all you have?" Ivy's jaw slacked.

"Intelligence said they knew where you lived. It

was a matter of time until you fell into their hands."

"Does this mean my parents are in danger, too?"

"Of course not. Where do you get this stuff?" he answered adorably. "TV?"

"I hope you weren't the one keeping Ms. Waters safe because we all know how that one turned out."

Molinar laughed. "There are strict rules for you to follow from this point on in order to remain alive. I'll explain those later."

"Rules? I don't like 'em, especially *strict* ones."

"I had a feeling you didn't." Ian said, "For the next few days, you'll be housed at headquarters. After that, you will go into hiding. Your location has already been chosen."

"Who chose it?"

"Me. It's my job to keep an eye on you and to keep you safe." He looked at her in the dark shadows of the car. "And just so you know, I wasn't the one watching over Ms. Waters."

Ian Serby got quiet. Ivy looked out the window. She hoped there'd be food at the end of the ride. Her hunger was growing. Candlelight and music would be a nice touch.

When she turned to ask Ian about stopping for food, he was pulling his fingers through his hair. He had gotten a hair cut since the last time she saw him but he wasn't used to it yet. It was then that Ivy noticed the ring on his finger. The music stopped and someone blew out the candle. Ivy couldn't help but feel guilty about her daydreams. She wondered about his wife. Did they do undercover projects together? And how was it, she could find a man who was married so incredibly fascinating? Her heart ached and she hated herself for feeling this way. But she also couldn't totally blame herself for her hope.

"I'm hungry," Ivy admitted scowling, thinking fast food wouldn't be fast enough to get away from Ian.

"We'll get you something to eat once we're at headquarters." Ian put away his notes and rubbed his chin with the back of his hand.

"Oh, I also need to get a prescription filled for my asthma."

"No worries. That has been taken care of. There are three containers already filled for you. When you need more, contact me."

"Wow, FBI agents think of everything," Ivy whistled.

He opened a ceiling compartment and took out a white pharmacy bag. "Put one in your purse now. Put the rest into your suitcase later."

Ivy looked inside of the bag and then set it on the seat beside her purse. "Thanks."

"You're welcome." Ian played with the gold and ruby band, spinning the ring around and around on his finger.

"I see you're married." Ivy looked at his ring finger again.

Now he looked at his ring as if forgetting he even had it on.

"All the good ones are taken." She smiled wistfully.

By the look on his face, Ivy wondered if he was going through a divorce. Now he spun his gold ring right off his finger. He went after it and put it back on. "This ring has been in my family for generations."

Ivy coughed.

"Do you need your inhaler?" Ian leaned forward filled with concern.

"No, I'm fine right now. Thanks for asking." Ivy saw him moving toward her in the darkness. He sat so close to her that his arm touched her skin making her feel protected, safe and yet at the same time making her want anything but safety—at least from him. She held back her urge to wrap her arms around him. The moment was electrifying, sending goosebumps over her arms. She closed her eyes being swallowed by this sense, allowing it to overtake her. After a few minutes, Ivy opened her eyes and looked up to find Ian's eyes focused on her.

"Ian?" She had to know if he felt anything for her at this moment. It was wrong but she couldn't keep herself from wanting him.

"Ivy, never react to any situation emotionally. I survived all these years because I remained in the shadows and kept my emotions in check. It would behoove you to do the same."

Minutes later a popping sound pinged against the car. Reflexively, Ian wrapped his arms about Ivy and rolled with her onto the floor of the vehicle. He covered her body with his. "Men, we're under fire." His voice was calm. More pings hit the car followed by deafening firepower.

Ivy didn't think she could hold it together and began hyperventilating. "Breathe evenly and count. Cool head, Ivy."

Roebuck swore. Molinar kept driving. With more rounds rattling off the metal, the car soon careened out of control and spun. An interstate lamppost stopped it. Steam rose from the sides of the crumpled hood. The doors along the driver's side were totally unusable.

"Ivy?" Ian whispered in her ear.

"I'm all right, Ian."

Molinar radioed the police and then his headquarters. His voice kept stopping and he gasped for air between his words. It was obvious he was hurt. Then the back door swung open and someone shot several times into the interior.

By the sound of his moan, she knew Ian was hit. His blood ran into the folds of her neck and down onto her chest. She bit her lip hard but didn't move. Then there were police sirens and swearing coming from someone outside the car. Wheels squealed away.

Within minutes a battery of Cook County police cars surrounded them. Someone lifted Ian out of the vehicle and laid him on his back on the interstate. Agent Roebuck helped Ivy from the floor of the backseat asking if she was all right. The streetlight revealed Ian's chalky face, his chest slowly rising and falling. Ivy knelt beside Ian. "I hear ambulance sirens. Help is on the way, Ian; please hang on."

"Ivy..." he choked.

"I'm here."

"Listen to me, Ivy. I was not following you, not at first. I was following Erin."

"Erin? I don't understand."

"You were right about the apartment. I was watching you there...to keep you safe...you are in terrible danger. They're coming for you," Ian lifted his eyes to hers.

"Who's coming for me?" Ivy felt her soul fill with fear.

"Sleep with your eyes open and stay in the shadows. Be strong. You can do it." He smiled thinly.

Ivy squeezed his hand. "I can't. I can't do this without you, Ian. I want to go home."

"You can do this. Things are not what they always seem to be." His face creased with pain. He took off his ring and pressed it into her hand. "Keep this for me..."

"Ian..." she cried.

Ambulances arrived. Paramedics began their work starting with the fallen agent. Ivy felt numb. She could no longer think. Garbled voices were speaking. They wanted her to do something, what was it?

"Release his hand! You've got to get out of the way so we can do our work!" someone yelled at her.

How is that done? Try as she may, her hand held

tightly on to Ian's hand. She felt safe. If she let go, then she may not be safe any longer. She'd die. Her hand simply wouldn't free his. A medic said more unintelligible words and then touched a pressure point in Ivy's wrist, making her release Ian's hand. She leaned back on the pavement, looking up at the night sky. It hurt her eyes. Why? Maybe it was the streetlight. Too bright.

Ivy watched as an IV was fed into Ian's veins. He was lifted onto a stretcher and strapped down. Paramedics surrounded him, and she couldn't tell if he was getting CPR. She wanted to go with them but she couldn't move. All she could do was watch helplessly as the stretcher with Ian on it was rolled into the ambulance. The doors slammed shut. More lights. There were more sirens, too. Ivy remained on the pavement but Ian's ring was still pressed tightly inside of her left palm. She found she could move just enough to slide it onto her middle finger. It fit there nicely.

"This is a crime scene and this woman is our sole witness. Why is she left alone like this! Would a medic please take a look at her?" Mitchell hollered, having just arrived by helicopter.

A paramedic sat on the ground next to her and checked her vitals. "She's going into shock. I think we'd better overnight her at the hospital."

Ivy looked heavenward, *I am in really big trouble this time.*

Chapter Nine

They took Ivy to a private Chicago hospital.

Close to unconsciousness, Ivy was only faintly aware of the shuffling of busy feet circling the table where she lay. White curtains had been pulled around her. It felt surreal as if she were floating, living in a parallel world. Someone called her by name, "Ivy! Can you hear me?"

"Ian?"

"Hello, Ivy. You are at Sterling Hospital in Chicago and I'm a doctor here. I am going to give you an injection of a drug that should help you feel better in a hurry. Do you understand what I am saying to you?"

Ivy shook her head affirmatively. The needle pierced her skin; the liquid oozed into her vein burned. She opened her mouth to complain but no sound came out. Trapped in a fog, her reactions were nonexistent; her mind muddied. Something was wrong. Something terrible had recently happened and it made her sad. Ivy tried to remember what that was. She wanted to focus her mind to figure it out.

"As soon as your vitals stabilize, you'll be taken to a room for the night. By tomorrow, you will be well enough to travel."

Moments passed. Ivy could open her eyes now. She stared up at the ceiling tiles. Someone was talking; she turned her head and saw there were a doctor and a nurse in the room. They noticed her staring at them and the doctor took a step toward her. "Hello, Ivy. Glad to see you are fully awake. I told you the drug worked fast."

Ivy tried to recollect how she got here. Then a memory emerged. She had been with someone. An FBI agent. His name was Ian and he was taking her to Chicago to speak with Rob. No, that was wrong. He was taking her to Chicago to keep her safe. Yes, that was it.

Something awful happened on the way. Maybe she really didn't want to remember what it was. Maybe it was better to return to the fog where there were no memories of anything.

Ivy closed her eyes. Images of Ian flickered through her mind. In one she was handing him her business card. It made him smile. Then she saw him in an apartment reading a fortune cookie. There he was again in her hometown of Twin Lakes but he was walking along the shallows of Lake Mary. Now they sat together in a car. He was telling her something. It was important; why couldn't she remember it? Another flash and Ian was lying on the pavement bleeding.

"No!" Ivy sat up with a jolt. Her hands covered her face as she tried to block out the terrible memory. It hurt to remember. Ivy felt Ian's ring on her finger. She looked at it and then remembered everything with clarity. Ivy moved the ring to her thumb and curled her fingers around it. No one was allowed to see it. If they knew about it, they might take it away and then she'd have nothing of Ian.

"Please, lay back down because we don't want to have to tranquilize you again." The nurse adjusted the blood pressure band around her forearm and took her pulse and temperature.

"Can you tell me what happened to the agent who was brought in tonight? I think two were brought in. Their last names are Serby and Molinar."

"Sorry, we haven't seen them. They may have been taken to another hospital."

"Can you ask someone for me, please? It's really important. I have to find out how they are, especially Special Agent Ian Serby."

"Just relax," the nurse told her as she wrote on the chart. By the look on the nurse's face, Ivy was certain she wasn't about to ask anyone about anything. She'd find out on her own. Hospitals had desks. Desks had phones. She'd call all the hospitals in a fifty-mile radius and fan out from there if she had to.

Ivy moved one leg and then the other. She pushed herself to a sitting position and dangled her feet over the side, gaining her balance. Just as she was about to step on the floor, the nurse yelled, "Whoa, young lady. Just where do you think you are going?"

"I told you, I need to find out about my friends, Agents Serby and Molinar. If you're not going to help me, then I will do it myself."

"The best thing right now is for you to rest." She gently pushed Ivy back, pulling the sheet up tightly around her neck as if that was enough to hold her in place.

Like a good patient, Ivy remained, noticing for the first time she had been stripped of her clothes and was garbed in a hospital gown. Ivy panicked. She needed her own clothes. It had all her money. Ivy looked around. There at the far end of the room she saw them. Her clothes appeared to be in a large plastic bag in the corner; she hoped no one thought to go through her pockets.

The doctor returned. "I just checked with the agents who have been assigned to your case. They say there is no news about either of your friends yet, sorry."

"There was a third agent…Roebuck. He was

there, too, but I'm not sure if he was hurt or not. Maybe you could ask for him," Ivy pleaded. "I know…can you get a hold of Agent Mitchell? He was the one in charge of securing the scene."

"Later." The doctor read her chart. "Good, it seems all systems are back to normal." Then he took a light from his pocket and checked her pupil reflexes. "I think you're ready to be taken to your room. I can do that since we're short staffed this evening."

The doctor helped Ivy into a wheel chair. Then he rolled her right past the bag containing her clothes and out into the hall.

"Hold on, I need that." Ivy pointed back into the room at the bag.

"Housekeeping has been notified and they're all ready on their way. Don't worry. By the time you're dismissed from the hospital, your clothes will be returned to you."

"No, I do not want them laundered. I insist on taking them with me now."

The doctor frowned. "It's really not sanitary."

"Please," she begged. "After all it's my stuff. You have no right to do anything with it without my permission."

The doctor was clearly agitated. Finally, he capitulated and placed the bag on her lap. He pushed Ivy in the wheelchair into the elevator, pressing the button for floor five. The doors closed.

"This hospital is different than the others I have seen. It's dead silent and you seem to be under-staffed."

"We do have our busy times," the doctor answered.

"It feels like I am the only patient in the whole place."

He didn't respond. The elevator doors opened and the doctor wheeled her down the waxed floors and into a room. It was good to see that her suitcase and her purse were already there. Ivy prayed the contents of both were left untouched.

"Security will be outside your door all night."

"That's reassuring," Ivy said as she climbed into bed.

"That, and the sleeping pill I ordered for you, will ensure a peaceful night's rest. The nurse will be bringing it in a few minutes." The doctor left her alone.

As far as she could tell, she was on an isolated floor and figured it was for security reasons. Here she'd be safe from the people who killed Ian. Ivy tugged at the scratchy hospital gown trying to see out the window, desperate to get her bearings. It dawned on her that she could be within walking distance of Congressman Gram's campaign headquarters.

The plastic bag was left on the floor. Ivy got out of bed and pulled at the fat knot at the top. She worked her fingers through the layer of plastic and got it untied. Ivy turned the bag upside down and dumped the contents onto the floor. She searched through the pockets. When she found the money was still intact she wanted to cheer.

Ivy scooped it up and carried it into the bathroom. Behind the closed door, she stacked the cash neatly together wondering what to do with it while she took a shower. There were no cabinets to slip it into. Everything was so out in the open; not even a curtain on the shower door. If someone walked in to check on her they'd see the cash first thing. For now she'd use her nightgown as a camouflage.

Satisfied with the concealment of the money, Ivy stepped into the shower, ready to take the fastest shower in her history. She cranked on the valve full blast. The beating of the water felt wonderful as she ran her fingers along her scalp, scrubbing with the sample bottle of shampoo she found in the bathroom. The coagulated blood began to loosen and run from her hair down onto the floor of the shower and out the drain. The sight of it made her nauseous. Anger, fright, and fury all welled and she couldn't help but sob uncontrollably. She cried until she felt she would die from pain. Ivy turned off the water and wrapped one towel around her body and another around her head.

Dripping with water, Ivy tracked her wet footprints from the bathroom to the bed. She opened her suitcase. She set Ms. Waters' book inside the table that was next to her bed. Tony's hard drive was harder to dig out since it was on the bottom. When she pulled it out, it rumpled all the clothes in her suitcase. It was important to be neat. With no control in her life right now, she'd make sure her suitcase was tidy. After she hid the hard drive with the other items, she refolded all the clothes, but kept out a pair of beige slacks and a white non-descript blouse to wear in the morning. Then she returned to the bathroom where she plucked up her cotton nightgown and slipped it over her head, and zipped back up her suitcase and set it on the floor.

As she looked for her inhaler, Ivy noticed a slice of light from the corridor underneath the door. Shadows began to move. If the FBI became aware of her money she was certain they'd hold it while they were holding her. No one would limit her options.

Any minute she expected the door to open and an agent to check on her or the nurse with her pill. Ivy got the money from the bathroom and put the wad into her purse. Ivy slid it under the bed.

Muffled voices in the hallway raised her curiosity. Hopefully, they had news about Ian and the other agents. Ivy cracked open the door and stepped out. There they were at the end of the hall with their backs toward her. One agent she didn't know but the other was Mitchell. What a relief, he'd know. Just then Mitchell said, "Serby is dead. He died on the way to the hospital."

Ivy's knees buckled.

"I hear Molinar is in surgery expected to make a full recovery. Roebuck wasn't hit," the other agent said.

"It's too bad the girl isn't dead. You were supposed to shoot both Ian and the girl," Agent Mitchell scolded.

The floor seemed to drop out from beneath her feet. Ivy could hardly take in what she was hearing. The men who were supposed to protect her wanted her dead. The FBI was her enemy. They murdered Ian. Now they aimed their sites on her. She felt an asthma attack coming on. Ivy quickly turned on her heels and slipped back into her room unnoticed. She mistakenly left the door open and heard them continue with the conversation.

"No worries. Very soon Ivy Dillon will have her own little accident but it can't be tonight under our watch. Her death has to look accidental."

"Good evening, Agents," the nurse greeted them as she stepped from the elevator.

Ivy quickly closed the door and jumped into bed just in time. The nurse walked in, "Ivy, by the looks of the wet towels you left on the floor, I see you've taken a shower. Good. I have your sleeping pill with me."

No way was she about to take that pill. Not when assassins plotted her demise. "Actually, I really don't need this," Ivy refused. "It's been a harrowing day and it's completely tired me out."

"Doctor's orders." The nurse held out the medicine cup.

"Just set it on the table. If I can't get to sleep, I'll take it then."

"No, I have to see you take it. When you arrived at the hospital this evening, you were traumatized. For a full recovery, you need to sleep soundly. Your body needs to repair itself. Go on and take it." Reluctantly, Ivy put the pill into her mouth but she cheeked it. As Ivy drank the water, the nurse added, "There are two agents stationed right outside your door watching over you. Early tomorrow, they'll be taking you to a safe house. So you have nothing to worry about. Have you swallowed your pill?"

Ivy nodded.

The nurse took Ivy's blood pressure, temperature, and pulse. Then she made notations of her vitals on the chart. All the while Ivy was quite aware of the bitter taste of the pill slowly dissolving inside of her mouth. At last, the nurse turned out the overhead light and left.

No sooner had the door shut, than it opened again. It was Mitchell, her pseudo-protector who plotted her death. He tiptoed around in the dark with only the outside streetlamp serving as his light. Ivy pretended to sleep. Breathing hard, she deliberately snored while peeking out with one eye. When the door shut again, Ivy waited for a moment to be sure no one else would come bursting into her room. Ivy sat up and looked around. The suitcase was gone. She sighed with relief, thankful she had taken out the most important items.

Immediately, Ivy spat out the pill. A bit of it had melted inside of her mouth. She worried that it was enough to make her groggy, but no way was she going with those agents anywhere tomorrow. She was leaving tonight. Right now. Every minute counted.

As Ivy knelt to pull her purse out from under the bed, she felt the effects from the trace elements of the pill she absorbed. A bit woozy she willed herself to work fast. Ivy divided the money into two sections. The first half stayed in the bottom of her purse. She stacked the hard drive on top and next went Ms. Waters' book.

After Ivy changed into her clean clothes, she tore her nightgown into long strips to fashion a money belt. She laid the second half of the money lengthways and then folded the material over and over again. Once it was wrapped around her waist she pinned the ends securely. If her purse was stolen, she wouldn't lose everything.

There was a half empty inhaler in her purse. The extra inhalers were still in the car. Why hadn't she done as Ian told her and put them into her purse right then? She sure couldn't ask anyone for them now. She needed to run away, down the hall, out the building, across the street, anywhere far away.

Ivy slid the purse strap over her shoulder and put the base of the purse under her arm for greater protection. She tossed her cell phone into the trash. It wasn't any good since she would be traced by the pings it would give off.

It was a gutsy move, but Ivy opened the door and looked up and down the hall. Thank goodness, the agents had taken a break. With no one in sight, she closed the door behind her with as little sound as humanly possible and moved like a shadow toward the exit stairs. Inside the stairwell, she ran down the five flights. When her feet hit bottom, there was a door that led directly to the outside. Ivy paused thinking it could be locked or set with an alarm. There was no other way out without retracing her steps. No way was she going back so she braced for a loud alarm and was slightly surprised when none sounded. She didn't kid herself though because she wasn't taking any chances of slowing down in case there was a silent alarm.

Chapter Ten

She thought she had all ready used up all her courage, but simply by stepping out onto the street, a whole new rush of bravery energized her. Ivy looked up and down the block. The heaviest traffic seemed to be flowing in an easterly direction so that was the direction she chose. Hide in plain sight. Hurrying along she gave sideways glances to the vehicles that passed her, staying close to the buildings so no one could snatch her. It was tempting to find Erin, but she knew they'd look there for her. She was certain they'd watch her parent's house, too. Ivy needed to think of someone so distant and some place so remote, that no one would suspect her to run there. That's when Gus, the retired White House security officer, came to mind.

Ivy was on a bus heading south to New Orleans before she knew it. She looked out the window with her arms wrapped tightly around her purse. Before they were out of the city, Ivy was sound asleep. By the time dawn's light appeared on the horizon, she was only a few hours from her destination.

The owner and cook of a popular new Creole business, Gus was easy to locate. Not only was he listed in the phonebook but everyone on the lakefront told her Gus's place was on the water right across from City Park. Ivy felt hideous after traveling for so long but for now that couldn't be helped. She took a seat at the back of the small restaurant and watched for Gus. A skinny teen with a white apron tied around his waist came up to the table for her order.

"Please tell Gus there is someone here from Washington for Jambalaya."

The kid nodded and disappeared into the kitchen. In a few minutes, Gus walked out, whistling a bouncy song but stopped when he saw Ivy. He slid into the booth across from her. It wasn't the reunion she had imagined. Gus wasn't smiling.

"I hear this place serves the best Cajun food," Ivy began. "It's good to see you."

"It's good to see you, too, Miss Dillon. Anything you want is on the house." He stared into her eyes. "But if I were you, I'd eat fast and be on my way."

"Then you know I'm in big trouble," Ivy's voice caught in her throat.

"Yup, that's right. People were here just an hour ago looking for you, showing your picture all around."

"FBI?"

"Don't think it was them." Gus shook his head. "But they looked tough."

Ivy bit her lower lip doing her best not to cry. "I came here hoping you could hide me. At least for a little while." She looked down at Ian's family ring and twisted it around on her finger.

"It's not safe for you to stay here, not for either of us."

Ivy started to get up.

"Just sit." Gus ordered. He leaned forward to pry his wallet out of his back pocket.

Ivy reached over the table and closed his wallet. "Gus, I don't need your money. I need your help."

Gus thought for a minute and then took keys from his front pocket. "Take my truck. It's not much but its right out front and it's all yours. Wait here while I'll fix you some food to take along." Gus laid the keys in front of her.

Ivy watched him go back to the kitchen. She got up and went out through the back door of the eatery, leaving the keys behind. For two days, she had pinned her hope on Gus and now she realized how silly that had been. Of course, he wouldn't put himself out there for someone he casually knew. From now on she had only herself to depend on if she were going to survive. Paranoid with good reason, she kept looking back all the way back to the bus station. At the counter, she asked for a ticket on the first bus out of the city. She was shaking as she boarded a bus for Texas.

****

Ivy traded one bus for another.

When she dozed, she cradled her head in her hand and felt the ring against her cheek. It brought back the safe feeling she had when she was with Ian. When she felt she couldn't ride another mile, she stepped off and found herself in Austin. With not one but two universities, she figured it was as good a place as any to hide. Among the thousands of students in a sprawling city, it was made to order for anyone who wanted a fresh start or remain anonymous. She'd merge right in as whoever she needed to be, for however long she needed invisibility.

It was late August with the temperature in the triple digits. The heat was debilitating, but hell's kitchen just might prove to be her safe haven.

Eating stale food from vending machines and not able to wash for days, Ivy felt ripe. She yearned for a cool shower and a fine meal to settle her stomach. Her skin ran with perspiration as she walked the streets of the campus looking for a place to eat. There were too many choices but she finally decided on a small diner.

It was a funky place packed with college kids snacking on thick hamburgers and sizzling fries. She found an empty seat at the counter and placed her purse firmly on her lap, squeezing into the counter in order to help protect all she owned. Barely out of college, she knew the system. Ivy guzzled the tall glass of ice water the waitress set in front of her, asking for two more before she felt she had a handle on cooling down. After she finished off a taco salad, she found the University Center and read the information boards for postings from people who wanted a roommate. She chose a rooming house, with her own room. Only a few blocks from campus, it was perfect but expensive. She gave a bogus name and then paid for a few nights stay. It was important not to put down too much in case she decided to pick up and go.

After she washed up in the room's sink, Ivy dropped face first onto her bed where she slept for over twelve hours. She dreamed of Ian. He was alive and they were together. She'd gladly give away all her money just to hear his voice one more time. But he was dead. Just like Karin. Just like Ms. Waters. The bodies were piling up around her.

When Ivy woke, she was hungry again but felt too frightened to leave her room. She stayed put, locked away in the room. Ivy sat cross-legged, hands clasped together in prayer. Emotionally drained, she fell back asleep.

Twelve hours later she got up enough courage to try the streets. It was good to be outside again. Ivy discovered that the city had a great bus system that not only traveled throughout all of Austin but also reached the burbs and to a dozen strip malls along the I-35 corridor.

Since everything she owned was over a thousand miles away and being pawed through by agents, she needed new clothes. Ivy rode a city bus to one of the malls. It was time to shake up her wardrobe. Cotton and polyester blends seemed the best choice and they all reflected the mood of the 1970s. While it wasn't her first choice, it seemed to be a popular style around here. Ivy also bought a denim satchel. In the mall's bathroom, she shoved her bag down into the trashcan. It would be a red flag to anyone driving the streets trying to find her. Now that she was in hiding, she needed to think of the smallest details in order to remain safe. Slip-ups could be deadly.

Next Ivy went to a bookstore for a couple of fashion makeup magazines and also the book she had gone to buy the day she ran into the Oliver family. It was in paperback now. A reminder of how time kept clipping right along. Then she ate again at the food court before she headed back to the bus stop with her purchases.

By mistake, Ivy didn't get off the bus at the right stop. As best as she could figure, she had waited too long and was blocks away from her rooming house.

But her mistake was proving to be a good thing when she saw a drug store and decided to stop in for a map of the city. While there she made additional purchases of several different shades of foundation along with eyeliner, blush, mascara, lipstick, hair dye, red-rimmed glasses, scissors, and a small radio. After a good look at the map, Ivy juggled her packages and kept her purse tucked as she angled her way down the streets.

She walked beneath the soft evening shade of crepe myrtle and mimosa trees, passing by a few homeless men along her way. Although she had sidestepped them back in Washington, Ivy could now feel pangs of compassion for them. In a few blocks, she saw another homeless man parked in the doorway of a business that was closed for the night. His plumber's crack was shocking and way past the point of no return, but thankfully, he leaned back on it as Ivy passed him. Ivy remembered the extra ten she had stuck down into her pocket and knew she could reach it fairly easily. Ivy quickly handed the man the bill.

He sang out, "Oh, God is so good...Thank ya, Jesus...Thank ya, Lawd." Then he fixed his eyes on Ivy's face. "Bless ya...may God bless ya and keep ya safe." He pulled himself up, hiked up his pants and hobbled down the street toward an all night café. Ivy turned back in the direction she needed to go, and within minutes, she had passed through the front doors of her rooming house.

It was beyond icky to share the one hallway bathroom with everyone on that floor but her choices were nonexistent at the moment. Ivy scoured out the filthy tub and took a long bath. She was just getting out when someone pounded on the door. Ivy threw on her clothes, frantically gathering her items. She pushed by the coed and hurried back down the hall to her room.

Ivy leaned over the room sink and cut her long locks off to chin length and cut pageboy bangs. She carefully read the directions on the box and then dyed her red hair to dark brown. She left it on for twenty minutes before rinsing out the color. Ivy cleaned up the mess and towel-dried her hair. She laid out her new makeup along the edge of the sink. According to the magazine she had propped open in front of her, it was important to wear base and powder in complimentary skin tones. The new red-framed glasses finished the new look. Now she was ready for a new life. Pleased with her new look, she washed her face and changed into her nightgown. In bed she held onto Ian's ring like a life preserver and listened to music on the radio. When romantic songs played, Ivy closed her eyes and dreamed of Ian. She imagined them sitting at the table back in his apartment and she poured her heart out to him, telling him about the strange hospital and how easily she had escaped.

Ivy held her hand up and looked at his ring. She couldn't help but think it looked like a wedding ring but he never actually said he was married. He did say it was a family ring passed down to him. It was bittersweet to know that it meant something to him, and as he was dying, he wanted her to have it. If only they had had more time.

The music on the radio stopped as the weather forecast started. The comfortable bed and the droning voice lulled Ivy into a bit of twilight zone until a disturbing newscast brought her fully awake again.

Chapter Eleven

"The FBI has issued an arrest warrant for Ivy Dillon who escaped their custody several nights ago in Illinois when she was brought in for questioning about the murder of the Presidential secretary, Geneen Waters. There is strong DNA evidence connecting Ms. Dillon to the murder and she is considered armed and dangerous. If you should see this fugitive, do not try to apprehend her yourself. Contact the authorities."

Numb with fear, Ivy slid on a pair of jeans and a top, and then took the stairs down to the lobby where the TV was blaring loudly to a room of empty chairs. Ivy wanted to hear more details so she scanned the channels and stopped when she saw her face on the screen. It wasn't a flattering picture with her hair caked in blood and her eyes wide with fear. She looked nutty and any reasonable juror would find her guilty based on that snapshot alone. Fortunately, the woman in the picture looked nothing like the one watching the clip.

Next was some psychiatrist by the name of Doctor Berg who claimed to have extensively examined Ivy Dillon shortly before her escape. His diagnosis of her was that she had a social personality disorder. Well, that flaky picture of her on the news sure confirmed his diagnosis even though she had never laid eyes on the man.

The anchor returned, grim-faced. "Days ago, Dillon reportedly stole a truck in Louisiana, but by now, she could be anywhere." Ivy mused sourly over another lie. Then realizing where she was, and frightened someone might suddenly walk into the room, Ivy hurried back to her own. Behind the locked door, she wrote a long letter to her family declaring her innocence. It was important for them to know her side, but mailing this letter without giving away her location posed another problem that would take a while to figure out.

She rechecked herself in the mirror above the dresser. The female looking back was nearly unrecognizable. *Very nice.* Then she remembered once seeing a TV segment about how easy it was to get a new identity. Ivy sat on the bed and made a list of things she recalled on how to acquire the needed identification. Tomorrow, she'd start on hers.

Ivy slept in till ten a.m. and then took a taxi to the outskirts of town where there was a large cemetery. She spent the rest of the morning and into the afternoon walking up and down the lanes in between the graves, reading headstones. Then she came to the grave of a girl who was born a few years before her birth date. Shelby Andrews only lived a few days before she died so no social security number would have been issued. Ivy decided to temporarily use her name. "Hello, Shelby Andrews. I need your name for a little while." Ivy wrote down her birth date, month and year on a scrap of paper.

It was getting late and there wasn't any sign of a cab in the area. Ivy began walking hoping to find a city bus stop. She was caught off guard by a toot of a horn. She looked inside the cab to see the same cabbie who dropped her here hours ago.

"Hey, need a ride back?" he asked.

"Thank goodness, I was worried all the cabs were on the other end of town for the night." Relieved, Ivy got into the backseat.

"Did you properly grieve?" the cabbie asked pulling out into traffic.

"I beg your pardon."

"I thought people went to the graveyard to grieve over a lost loved one, but it's none of my business what you were doing there," he said.

"I did spend time at a few graves." Ivy didn't want to say more.

"Where to now, miss?"

"I need to find a mail store and get a post box number. Do you know where one is within walking distance of the University?"

"I sure do." The old geezer was quite helpful. When he dropped Ivy off, she paid him his fee and added a good tip. Once inside the store, Ivy rented a box for six months and now she had a real address of her own, even if it was the number and street of the store location.

Next Ivy found the Social Security office to tell her rehearsed story. Fortunately, she told it to a sympathetic male who fell for her line of being born at home and then raised by a father whose religious beliefs didn't include social security numbers. Now that she was older, she left her old-fashioned home to find work so she could finally be on her own. Giving her mailbox and that street location as her address, she was credible. In a few weeks, she'd have her new social security card which would allow her to apply for her driver's license and credit cards. It was too easy. That's what worried her.

In spite of her worry, Ivy Dillon was reborn as Shelby Andrews—at least for the time being.

****

Shelby's newest piece of identity was a library card. It was the key to surfing the net for additional news about the ongoing investigation of Ms. Waters' murder and the country-wide manhunt for her. No matter how tempted she felt, she didn't go into the FBI website just in case it was used for tracking criminals who looked themselves up.

By now, her parents had to be wild with worry especially with all the news coverage. The last time they saw her, she was leaving in the dead of night with a pack of strangers in a dark sedan. Every night, Shelby lay across her bed and wrote home. In a month, she had a large mailer filled with letters. Shelby suspected her parent's mail might be screened. She printed her parent's name in block letters and the neighbor's address right beneath it, with a bogus return address at the top left-hand side. Hopefully, the neighbor would hand carry it next door to her folks. No way could she send it from Austin. The postmark would be a bull's-eye to finding her.

Shelby took a bus to Dallas and then into Oklahoma. During the next bus ride into Colorado, she read a few magazines she had picked up at the last stop and paged through the book on Egypt. She tried to sleep but her back hurt from sitting so long. Someone at the back of the bus sang Amazing Grace. The voice was lousy but the words were soothing. Tears sprang to her eyes. This wasn't the time for them so she tried to blink them back. They kept coming. Finally, she gave into her emotions and let them come. It felt like a rain that swept away her mistakes. Ian was dead. No one else could help her. Except her. *My parents raised me to be strong and I can do this.*

Shelby looked at the ruby ring on her finger, making a promise that someday she'd find his family and return it to them. In the meantime, she would treasure it.

There out the bus windows were the majestic Rocky Mountains. Shelby left the station and headed in the direction of the post office. At the corner was a phone booth and she eyed it all the way down the street. More than anything, Shelby wanted to call home to hear her parent's voices but it wouldn't be long for agents from the Boulder office to descend on her. No way would she toss her freedom away in a flash of homesickness. Ian's dying words to her were to think with her head and not her emotions. Again, she felt the ring on her finger.

In the lobby of the United States Postal Office, Shelby went to the self-serve machine where she weighed the envelope and dropped her money into the machine. A printed postage tag came out which she affixed to the envelope and then kissed it once before slipping it into the mailbox. If it fell into the wrong hands, the postmark would put her far from her actual location. Mission accomplished, it was time to head back South. A few days later Shelby was back in the sweltering south Texas heat. Depression became an issue.

****

Shelby varied her daily routine. She took different routes to and from places she frequented. Unobtrusive traps were set outside her room at the rooming house. Going out, Shelby placed a piece of tape at the bottom edge from the outside of the door to the door jam. At night, a door alarm meant for use in hotel rooms was placed on the inside doorknob. If anyone even turned the knob from the outside of the room, the alarm sounded.

At first it was hard to simmer down about the possibility of being killed at any moment. It was hard to know how close anyone was to finding her. Ian had told her to sleep with her hands ready, which she did. Lying on her back each night, with her hands crossed over her chest, she'd be ready to fight off any attacker. But at night, it wasn't an attacker that visited her but thoughts of Ian. She tried to remember the exact curve of his cheek, the way his voice sounded when he handed her the ring, and that great smile of his that spread goosebumps along her arms. His green eyes would always be her favorite color.

At last, her new social security number arrived. The name Shelby Andrews was printed above a series of numbers. She stared at the card for a long time. Now she went to the DMV and applied for a driver's license. When she was handed the new card, Shelby felt as excited as she had when she turned sixteen and got it for the very first time. By Christmas, she had two credit cards in her name.

Thankful the name had kept her safe, she yearned to return to her life as Ivy Dillon. Shelby could help her do that so that she could return to being Ivy and Shelby could return to the beautiful, peaceful resting place where Ivy found her. To do all of that, they needed to find out who killed Ms. Waters.

Spread out on her bed were all the identification cards. One by one she picked them up and slid them into a special section in her wallet. Shelby flipped through the TV channels, thankful for the satellite dish. She paused on the channel that showed a close-up of Robert Gram on the floor of Congress.

"I feel honored to be presenting here today before such a distinguished group of politicians. Today, I am introducing a new piece of legislation that will aid in the accuracy of counting votes electronically. I am sure it will become a popular bill for we all know how voting machines vary from state to state, from county to county, even from city to city." Gram turned and pointed to a short film illustrating what he was saying. On the screen were five different types of voting machines. Then it faded to black as the camera refocused on the newly elected congressman.

He smiled but it was a weak smile that Shelby didn't like. "There are even some places where the voter uses a pen to mark their choices on a paper ballot and then on their way out of the precinct, they put that ballot into a box. When the box becomes too full, one of the proctors takes those votes out and puts them into a larger box."

Another short clip is shown with people stuffing the boxes with their ballots. Then there was a tight shot of an exasperated woman because there was no room in the box for her ballot.

Gram continued, "At the end of the day, a proctor goes through those ballots one by one and tallies up the votes." Now there was a shot on the screen of someone looking harried as they tallied with one hand and ran their fingers through their hair with the other. He yawns and looks sleepy.

"All these are outdated modes of voting. It adds to the distrust of the American people on Election Day. I propose we replace those old ways and bring America up to date. Every voting machine in every town, city, county, capital and state should have the exact same machine and the exact same way of voting. That way we can rest assured that every person has cast his or her vote accurately, that every man and woman has been heard. Connected to these machines will be a microchip that will electronically tally and then send the results to one location in the mainframe. All the machines will be exactly the same." Wild applause followed.

Flipping through the TV channels again, she saw the answer to her prayers. There on leading news channel was none other than Sam Oliver.

****

Seeing Sam had given Shelby the push she needed to move to the next level. It was late spring and time to leave. Shelby slapped down $5,000 for the used car. With a new wardrobe in the trunk and a new driver's license, social security number, and credit cards in her purse, she drove out of Austin. It was time for Ivy to show Shelby the sites of Washington D.C.

Three days later, Shelby was in Virginia looking for places to stay when a yard sale sign caught her eye at *Dusty Trails Trailer Park.* A young woman wearing jeans for a second skin was just pricing her wares. Shelby walked around picking things up and then setting them carefully back down again.

"Is there anything special you're looking for?" the red-headed woman asked with a hand on her hip.

"Nothing in particular."

"You don't sound like you're from around here?"

"I'm new to Virginia," Shelby told her.

"Welcome. I'm Betty Lou," she held out her hand to Shelby.

"Shelby." She shook Betty Lou's hand.

There was an interesting looking cardboard box under one of the tables. Shelby squatted down and began to dig through it. To her delight, she found blue canning jars that still had their original milk glass lids.

"Those are old…" Betty Lou apologized.

"And aren't they wonderful? How much do you want for the entire box?"

"Is five dollars too much?"

"Five dollars is fine." Shelby paid her the cash and then put the box carefully into the backseat and waved goodbye.

Shelby drove the back roads of Virginia until she came to the business street of Ashland, ninety miles outside of DC. It was a pretty little town with train tracks running down the middle of Main Street. Ashland was a conservative community of six thousand filled with businessmen wearing button-down shirts and women who spent their mornings watching their children play in the community park. A large sign announced their attitude as "Center of the Universe". It was as far as one could get from Austin's population and bohemian style.

On the corner was a realty company where a pretty African-American woman sat tending the front desk. Her feet were propped up as the hem of the terra cotta colored summer knit dress slid along her long slim legs. When she saw Shelby she quickly got to her feet, making her marvelous corkscrew curls bounce.

"May I help you?" she asked, showing off a pearly-white smile.

"Yes, I'm interested in renting a small house for about a year," Shelby answered.

"Follow me." Shelby followed the woman into a office decorated in earth tones. "I'm Jerrica Lincoln."

"That's an interesting name."

"Actually, it's based on an old tradition. In slave days most times, children were separated from their parents. To help keep their identity, they combined the first names of the parents. My parents carried on this little tradition with me. My dad's name is Jared and my Mom's name is Erica. I'm Jerrica."

"What a lovely tradition!"

"Thanks, now tell me about the kind of house you would like?" Jerrica slid a strand of hair behind her ear.

"I'm not planning to stay past a year so renting is best for me. I don't need anything large." Shelby sat primly in the chair with her hands folded together over her purse.

"That doesn't give me much to go on. Do you and your husband have any children? It'll mean more bedrooms for the kids, unless they like to share?" she said.

"No, I'm unmarried. No children."

"Should I offer condolences for not having them or congratulations for an unhampered life?"

Shelby laughed. "You're a character. I want a house with large square rooms and good light. One or two bedrooms would be enough. I prefer older homes and like the 'lived-in' feel. A shaded yard with morning sun for a vegetable garden. A front porch on the house would be nice so I could sit out there in the evening." Her own words surprised Shelby. Last night she would have settled for a two-room walk-up but now today, she wanted a home with a garden like her mother's back home.

"I have the perfect house for you. We'll ride over together in my car."

Shelby followed Jerrica to her car. Minutes later, they stopped in front of a weathered cottage put together with clapboard siding and hammered rose head nails. Only a speck of it could be seen from the street as it was beautifully hidden behind perfectly shaped shrubs and garden trellises. Shelby walked through the iron gates, opened the blue painted door, and walked into the house. It was just as she hoped with old wood floors, wainscoting on the walls and crown moldings; a wave of perfect well-being engulfed her.

The backdoor opened up into a Garden of Eden of sorts, with profusely blooming Foxgloves, antique roses, ivy, peonies, lilies, hydrangeas, among the dozens of flowers and spiky shrubs. Weeds were overdue for a pulling, along with flowers that had turned brown from the chilly nights. "The garden needs some serious help. As soon as we get our first frost in late November, most of it will go dormant." Jerrica stood with her arms crossed over her chest, a light wind ruffling her hair.

"Nice breezes come down from the Blue Ridge Mountains in the evening." Jerrica pointed toward the west. "You'll get a panoramic view of fall colors when frost hits the mountains in early September. This rental has been empty for a year, as if it's been waiting for you."

"I believe it. I belong here." Shelby plopped down on an old rocker on the front porch, feeling as if she had come home after a long journey.

"Well, here's the key." Jerrica offered, "You can move in right away. The rent is due the first of every month."

With those words, the cottage belonged to Shelby. With only clothes to hang in the closets and underwear to slip into drawers, it didn't take long to settle into the place. She filled her garage sale jars with flowers from the garden including sweet peas, daisies, lupines, and Black-Eyed Susans. It made her feel that she was adding her own special touches to a place which already seemed perfect for her.

The next day, Shelby purchased a laptop and a laser printer. Now she was ready to catch up on the investigation. With a box of folders and plenty of paper, she began building her files in a dossier box. Not sure what was valuable to the case, she decided to print everything about the murder and build a hard-copy history. It turned into her nighttime entertainment. She needed something to occupy her thoughts now that she finally accepted Ian's death.

She circled in red and highlighted in yellow points she didn't understand or refuted. While she was in the organizing mood, Shelby categorized the bits of research she pulled off the net. What she found was intriguing and went a long way to explaining the reason she was accused. It made her be grateful to still be alive.

It was hard to read a report or see a picture of Ms. Waters without dissolving into tears. One picture was of particular interest to her. It was the spot along the bank of the Potomac River where the body was found. She had come to an ignominious, horrifying end. Of course, her body had been removed by the time this particular photo was taken, but it was a chilling reminder of her demise. Shelby put away her paperwork and turned off the reading light overhead.

Chapter Twelve

Day was breaking and it was time to find Sam. Dressed in a blue 70's style polyester summer dress with white sandals on her feet, she pulled her dark hair away from her face. Sighing at herself in the mirror, she disliked this new color even more than the original red God had given her. Shelby put on makeup, altering her complexion to that of a middle-aged woman using a bit of latex which she had gotten from an acting store on campus and making sure she spread it along her hairline. She had watched Erin countless times use this stuff before going on stage and that knowledge came in handy today. Shelby then took off the headband and her hair dropped around her shoulders. She combed gray streaks through her hair with a new, temporary product recently out on the market and put on her red-rimmed glasses. She practiced walking in a stooped position so she was comfortable with it before heading out.

It was good to be back on familiar turf. Drinking in the memories and atmosphere, Shelby took her time and wandered the busy streets of Washington D.C. She stopped at a street cart to buy some lunch and then ate a fat, juicy hot dog on a bench in the park. Next she walked Capitol Hill and looked up the steps of the White House. At The Russell Senate building, a group of faceless bureaucrats huddled together in debate at the top of the stairs. One of them stepped back from the crowd and began his descent. There was something familiar about him and it made her heart jump from fear.

Robert Gram. He came down the steps right toward her with determination as if he recognized her. Adrenaline shot through Shelby's body making her light-headed and her hands prickly. Shelby glanced around wanting to hide. There across the street was a newsstand. Her instinct was to run for it, but an older woman sprinting across the pavement like a twenty-year-old would garnish too much attention and attention was not what she wanted.

Think with your head. Shelby ran her thumb over the gold ring and then crossed the street to the stand. Somewhat safer now, she peered around the corner to get a second look.

Congressman Gram remained at the bottom of the steps. The smart thing would be to get to her car and drive out of the city, but curiosity glued her to the spot. Rob looked at his wristwatch. A woman soon walked up to him. It was too far away to see her features but she pulled a manila folder from her attaché and handed it to him. Without looking at it, Rob put it inside his briefcase.

Overwhelmed by emotion, Shelby's hands began to shake. She put them up under her armpits trying to make them stop. An anxiety attack dropped over her. Feeling wheezy, she pulled her inhaler from her purse and used the last drop of medicine. She shook it violently just in case she could get one more blast from it, but it was no use. The medicine was done and it was only time until the big one hit. Shelby slipped the inhaler back into her pocket and looked at the couple again.

They appeared as if they were about to go in opposite directions. Hesitating they exchanged looks. The woman took Rob's arm and together they headed in Shelby's direction. Now only a few yards away and closing in fast, Shelby snatched a magazine to cover her face.

"Hey! Put that back where you got it." The vendor snatched it from her hands leaving her feeling naked and exposed—vulnerable.

Now the couple was within feet of her. The woman seemed familiar in her typical Washington establishment two-piece business suit. The woman's hair was cut in a fashionable pageboy just above her collar. Looking closer, without being too obvious, there was no mistaking those almond shaped eyes and beautiful face. It was Erin.

The couple was a yard away. They looked at her but it was as if she were a vapor because they brushed right passed. Shelby darted away in the opposite direction. Pushed by adrenalin, she hurried for blocks and only stopped to hail a taxi.

"Where to?" the cabbie asked once she was inside.

"Just drive for a little while." Shelby needed time to think. After a few minutes, she handed the cabbie the address of the location where Ms. Waters had gone into the Potomac. It took a while to reach the area, through the mid-day traffic. When they finally arrived, Shelby paid the driver and stepped out into a seedy neighborhood. With a squeal of tires, the cabbie peeled off down the street. She worried about getting a cab back to her car, but she couldn't think about it right now as she looked around.

Bars and abandoned buildings lined the streets. Loud music blared out from hidden sources. Stray cats and sickly dogs sniffed about trashcans. Shelby stood at the edge of the pavement and looked down into the undergrowth that led directly to the riverbank. Her 'men in black' had been correct in saying Ms. Waters never would have just fallen in the river here. In order to get to the river, you had to fight your way down to it. Shelby started her tricky walk through the briars and the stickweeds, stepping over litter. It was a difficult walk and she struggled for footing every inch of the way down the slope.

There were more obstacles to traverse before reaching her destination; cement barriers and a steep decline filled with more discarded paraphernalia like old motors and large bags of garbage. Even an old soiled mattress losing its stuffing was tossed here. No, Ms. Waters surely wasn't on an afternoon walk; she'd never come here.

At the riverbank, there was a large drum filled with thick brown sludge and rotting fish were scattered in the shallows. There was a picture of this location recently on the net and Shelby had printed it off. It was inside her purse so she pulled it out and held it up to compare. Yes, it was about here they found the body. It was horrifying that anyone would end up here.

Shelby clutched hold of gnarly vines and half dead bushes to help her along the way. Finally back at street level, she found herself panting hard and walked three blocks until she found another taxi to take her back to her car where she sat for several minutes praying to breathe easier. When she felt better, she started the car and aimed the air conditioning up into her face.

Her original intention today was to find Sam but now it was late and physically she was done in. However, there was no way she'd leave the city without scoping out the news building where Sam worked. She drove with one hand on the steering wheel while holding the address up in the other. As she cruised by the building, she craned her neck trying to see the faces going in and out of the glass doors. There was so much traffic her attention was divided. A policeman on foot hurried down the street toward her and hollered, "Move it! You're blocking traffic!"

God, HELP! Don't let me be caught!

****

The close call in traffic was enough to really send Shelby spinning. It was day number two of the big attack she knew would eventually come, especially with that kind of trigger. The last time she felt this badly she went to the emergency room, but that was three years ago when she could go as herself, Ivy Dillon. Today, Shelby could barely make it to the bathroom without leaning on the walls for support. All the gardening and her walk in D.C. had done her totally in. If it weren't for Jerrica bringing her food, she'd starve to death.

The doorbell pinged. Right on time, Jerrica breezed through the entry and into the living room. "Lunch again today, as promised," she held up the salad and placed it on the coffee table.

"Thanks. You're a true friend."

Jerrica stood with her hands on her hips. "I'm on my way to meet someone to show horse property. Call if you need anything, you hear me?"

"Will do, but I'll be fine."

"You don't look so fine." Jerrica touched her forehead. "Your face is paper white and your skin is clammy."

"Stop worrying Jerrica. I just need more rest."

"I'll check on you again this evening."

After Jerrica left, Shelby turned on the television and nestled down to try and get that rest. She hoped she was telling Jerrica the truth.

When Shelby awoke, she was in total distress. Her breath came fast and shallow. The room began to fade in and out, as beads of perspiration ran down the length of her body. Shelby looked down at her unsteady hands and could see that her nail beds had turned blue. She slid onto the floor and was barely able to reach the phone.

"Jer…rica, come. I…can't…breathe…"

"Shelby, we're on our way!"

****

At the emergency room, the doctor administered a bronchodilator and soon Shelby's throat opened up. Once she was stabilized, the doctor made preparations to release her.

"Here is a new inhaler, young lady. If this new brand works well for you, stop back and I'll write out a prescription."

"I appreciate it," Shelby answered, thankful to be given medicine while not ending up in some medical registry for a new prescription. She decided to only use it in extreme emergencies like the one she just experienced and vowed to stay out of the garden no matter how many weeds needed pulling. The weeds could go crazy in her backyard, if they wanted; she wouldn't even look. She had a close call and learned her lesson, one she wasn't anxious to repeat.

Shelby walked into the lobby where Jerrica anxiously awaited. Jerrica stretched out her arms and hugged her. "That was quick. Are you all right?"

"I am now, thanks. Sorry I frightened you."

"What did the doctor say?"

"He said I'm fine. I'm thankful for you, my friend. If it weren't for you coming to my aid, I don't know that I would have made it," she chided with a laugh which made her cough. "Let's get out of this joint. I want to go home to bed."

"I was with a client when you called. Shelby, this is Sam Oliver. He followed behind us to the hospital. Sam, I want you to meet my friend Shelby Andrews." Jerrica stepped aside and Shelby saw him for the first time since the bookstore in Washington.

Panic registered within and her instinct was to turn on her heels and return to the emergency room. For some reason, she couldn't unglue herself from the spot. "Hello, Mr. Oliver." Shelby's eyebrows shot up. She held out her hand to him and numbly shook his, all the while fearing he would recognize her and call her out on the spot.

"It's nice to meet you, Ms. Andrews." Sam narrowed his eyes. He appeared wary.

It made Shelby pull her bangs down over her eyes and comb hair over the sides of her face with her fingers.

"I was showing Sam property for raising Morgan horses when you called. He has a pair in a city stable that he is anxious to get moved. There's not enough room in the barn he has now. It's all ready full of horses," Jerrica explained.

"Do you ride, Ms Andrews?" Sam asked.

"I haven't ridden in years." Shelby kept her chin tucked figuring Sam may not recognize her if he didn't get a full view of her face. "Jerrica, would you mind taking me home now. I'm really quite tired."

"Of course, you are. Jerrica, take your friend home so she can get some rest." They walked toward the door as Sam continued, "Maybe you would like to go horseback riding with my son and me sometime, Ms. Andrews."

"As I said, I haven't ridden in years," Shelby demurred.

"If you change your mind, just let Jerrica know and she'll contact me. Drive carefully, ladies." Sam held the outside door for them and then sprinted ahead to his car.

On the way home in Jerrica's car, her friend commented, "Sam must be taken with you, Shelby. He practically asked you out on a date the moment he met you."

"What are you talking about? Sam is married and has a son. I can't imagine Sam's wife would appreciate hearing about his flirtatious ways."

"His wife? It's very sad; she passed away just

over a year ago."

"Sam isn't married?" Shelby gasped suddenly seeing a wide open field blossoming with hope. "I didn't expect that to happen."

"I am not sure what you're saying." Jerrica gave Shelby a sideways glance.

"He has a son, I just assumed…never mind." Shelby tried to act nonchalant but her jitters were a dead give-away that something more was going on. She had to cover or Jerrica might start asking questions she didn't want to answer. "So this is the guy, the great guy you want me to date? He seems really nice."

"He's great. And Sam has been lonely." Jerrica glanced toward her once again before softly continuing. "And if you don't mind me saying this, you seem rather lonely, too."

Chapter Thirteen

A week passed before Sam called Shelby to see how she was. The conversation was short and stumbling. Mainly, Sam told her about how his mare had a foal and what she looked like. Just as Sam started to say goodbye, Shelby stepped out in faith and invited Sam and Noah for lunch.

If only there was more time to straighten the place up. Magazines were spread across the large hassock and cascading onto the floor and well-read newspapers from all over the country were stacked on a table. She had her news research from the computer right out in the open and unwashed dishes gathered at the bottom of the sink.

Shelby opted for personal hygiene and took a shower. She pulled on clean jeans with a white cotton T-shirt and smeared on her makeup to hide Ivy. Then she slid the red-rimmed glasses onto her nose and brushed her hair down about her face. She then rushed to the kitchen to get rid of the dishes and flew around picking up the remaining items as best she could.

A moment later her doorbell rang. Sam's mouth twisted up slightly on one side with a smile when she opened her door to them. There on her doorstep was father and son. They both took off their boots and left them outside on the stoop.

Sam sat on an old painted kitchen chair. Noah was on another while Shelby sat across from them. They ate cold fried chicken and potato salad with thick rolls.

"Thank you for this delectable chicken," Noah said.

"Wow, 'delectable'. I'm so impressed with your big word, Noah," Shelby laughed feeling a bit jumpy. Even her knees were thumping together beneath the table.

"I do have an immense vocabulary for my age," the young boy admitted.

"Were you born to geniuses?"

"His mother was a member of Mensa," Sam explained.

"Then that explains it. I think you also got your hair color from your mom, Noah." She messed his curls. "What did you get from your dad?"

"A new truck." He pointed to the toy on her coffee table. "But I wanted a dog."

"Maybe next time you'll get one."

"Jesus will give me one if Daddy doesn't," Noah sighed confidently. "Can I go play with my truck, Dad?"

"Sure, you're excused," Sam said as he cleared the table.

Noah hopped down from his chair and scrambled over to his toy, immediately starting his truck noises as it rode over the furniture.

"You really don't have to do clean up. I can get them later."

"It's my way of thanking you for the impromptu meal."

Sam carefully wiped away the crumbs from the countertops. Suddenly, a growing change on his face caught her off guard. His smile turned downward and his forehead bunched up in furrows as serious thunderclouds gathered along his temples. An uneasy feeling crept in lodging in her heart; tension hung in the air between them for several minutes. Sam seemed irked. Had she been offensive?

Drying his hands, he asked, "How's your

asthma?"

"Fine. No more problem since the hospital but I'm staying out of the garden."

"That's good." He stared at her hard as he sat down in the chair across the table from her.

"Sam, what's wrong?"

"It's always nice to run into old friends, isn't it?" Sam looked up into her eyes.

Suddenly, she was dizzy as if the floor was dropping out beneath her. She touched the edge of the table with her fingers to steady herself.

"I'm not blind, *Ivy*."

Rattled by the sound of him saying her real name she staggered emotionally. So this is what it was all about. He had recognized her after all. Of course he would, why did she ever think dark hair and makeup would throw him off? Shelby touched her ugly, short brown hair. She felt ridiculous. She looked ridiculous.

"You've changed since the last time I saw you, but not enough to be another person. I've been waiting for you to tell me your side of the story, but my patience has worn thin. Somehow I can't see the girl I once knew on the FBI's ten most wanted list. You've a story to tell me and I want to hear it now. If you don't want to share, I'm not willing to go on pretending like this."

Quietly, Shelby slid into the chair opposite him. It was good to at last be with someone who knew her real identity. Now that the shock wore off, relief came. Even though they sat across the table, inches away from each other, there was a whole pile of history that separated them. Shelby felt like there were unreturned messages in her heart but she'd save those for later. Right now, Sam wanted answers about her criminal past. Hadn't she come all this way to enlist his help? Well, now she was about to find out if she'd get it.

"It's hard to believe that just over a year ago I was a White House Intern to the President's secretary..."

"Geneen Waters, who's been murdered." Sam was a step ahead of her, which didn't surprise her since he had reported the story.

Shelby lowered her voice not wanting Noah to hear, "But I didn't do it. You have to believe me."

"The FBI says you did."

"Someone is framing me. Ms Waters and I overheard a conversation at The White House. She went to the FBI about it and ends up dead. I am next."

"Whoa, back up. You overheard a conversation? What kind of a conversation?"

"Something about a Top Dog. Don't laugh, Sam. I know it sounds silly!"

"Top Dog?" He reacted with a startled jolt. "Did you recognize the voices?"

"Sam, you seem like you know something, what?"

"Just answer my question."

"I never saw their faces; they were in the conference room. I was out in the hallway, but I heard them arguing over lost software."

"And Ms. Waters was in the hall with you?"

She nodded.

"Any ideas about who murdered Ms. Waters?"

"No, but I think it was probably the same men who murdered FBI Special Agent Serby, and now, they are after me."

"An agent was murdered, too? This is huge." Sam glanced about the room. When he saw a pad of paper, he snatched it. "Anything to write with?"

Shelby pointed toward a mug filled with pencils and pens. Sam went through the pens, finding the one he wanted, he sat back down. "Okay, start this story of yours again."

While she filled Sam in on the events, she kept touching the ring. It helped her focus and remember details.

Sam asked, "What I can't understand now is why you weren't killed that night along with the agent?"

"Ian succeeded in his job to protect me."

"How did you get out of the hospital without being noticed?"

"It was surprisingly easy. I went for the exit. Then I took the stairs down and went out through a security door to the street."

"What about the alarm? Security cameras?"

"No alarm sounded and as for the cameras, I don't know about them." This didn't seem peculiar to her till now. But by the puzzled way Sam appeared, it wasn't good.

"That's strange. Alarms are set by hard wire and a timer. Someone would have to deliberately turn off the system on all the doors for one alarm not to sound. That can only be done with reprogramming the system and that probably is under lock and key."

"Why would someone want me to escape?"

"To get you out on the street. If something happened in the hospital, authorities would know it was an inside job," Sam figured. "You played right into their hands. However, you outsmarted them. Another option for your easy escape is that perhaps you have an anonymous friend in the agency who left that back door alarm turned off, hoping you'd use it. My first guess would be Agent Serby but since he's dead, we have to keep looking."

"One more thing, months ago, Rob Gram was on TV addressing the congress about new voting machines."

"Interesting, isn't it? I heard it, too. Until today, I viewed him as a fairly low-level, somewhat unpopular, play-it-safe type of congressman so I haven't paid much attention to him. But now he's on my radar. I'm going to do some investigating. I'll also see what I can find on this Ian Serby for you. Why didn't you just come to see me right away?"

A dam broke inside Shelby and words burst over the tumbling water. "Fear, confusion, hostility—pick one. I didn't want to intrude on your family. Plus, I was scared about being this close to Washington and wondered if you'd turn me over to the authorities. Then I got sick and one thing led to another and that led me to you. Here you are today, sitting at my kitchen table with your sweet little son asleep on the couch in the next room."

Sam turned in his chair and smiled broadly at his son who picked a comfy spot for an afternoon snooze. Small couch pillows had tumbled over on him. "I just wish you were direct with me from the start."

Shelby poured her heart out to him and in return he scolded her. "Of course, but it's easy for you to tell me what I should have done. You report the news while I seem to make it!"

"Oh no, do you still play the poor Ivy card when things don't go right? I thought maybe you had grown out of that," Sam was condescending.

Shelby bristled. "I first needed a plan. Forgive me; it took me a while to come up with one. Frankly, I was considering your wife's and Noah's feelings. There was no way I could just show up unexpectedly and knock on your front door, right? 'Hi, I'm Ivy Dillon, your husband's former fiancée. Presently, I'm running for my life. Is it okay if we sit down together in the den and talk about it? Oh, and by the way, would you please watch out the window for the FBI?' Anyway, I had no idea what street your front door was on."

"Grace is dead." His voice was strong and sad.

He used her name. He didn't say 'my wife.' He

used her name and, in the manner he said it, she knew he was deeply in love with her still. "I recently heard. I'm sorry. She must have been very special to have won you."

"Just when I begin to forget, I look at Noah and remember Grace with such clarity." Sam shuffled uneasily in his chair. "It's hard for me to talk about Grace to you."

She perched tentatively at the rim of her chair wanting to hear more. It would help resolve the past for her. "Just tell me, Sam. What was Grace like?"

"Grace was smart and kindhearted. Grace had this quick wit but she never used it to slight anyone. She knew me without holding my shortcomings against me. Then we had Noah. Our family was complete, perfect." Sam looked straight at Shelby. "Once I had it all."

"And while you wed this perfect woman, I'm alone."

"Poor Ivy is lonely and my wife dies. Not much of a competition there."

Shelby began to shake with fury. "You belittle my feelings and dismiss what you did."

"No, I hear you were rewarded for *not* following me to Washington."

"Now we get to the point. Tell me your perspective." Shelby slid toward the back of the chair and crossed one arm over the other.

"You did get the country house."

"That's right!" Now she clapped her hands together as her anger rose like a tide. "You let me have the ramshackle house. Thank you!"

"That's rather a tasteless comment."

"Here's another tasteless comment for you. You left for Washington to find a job and a place for us to live and ended up with a new bride. You never looked back. You never considered me."

"I did and didn't want to hurt you."

"Well, you failed miserably." Shelby laughed wildly. "Calling me on the phone was so insensitive. Did you know the very next day our wedding announcement was in the local newspaper? Breaking the news to the people in town was so painful that we finally took the phone off the hook. I couldn't leave the house for weeks without someone asking me about you. But the worst thing of all was taking your ring from my finger."

"Ivy…" The look on Sam's face told Shelby he was beginning to understand.

"Don't worry Sam. We were never meant to be together."

"Or we'd be married now." The words were spoken softly but were sharp enough to slice into her heart. Seeing Sam again made her stumble emotionally.

"I did love you, but when I met Grace that was it for me. I couldn't imagine my life without her. Now I have to live my life without her and I don't know how to do that."

"How did she die?" Shelby was pressing into painful territory but she had to know.

"Grace died very unexpectedly of an undetected condition. An aneurysm had formed near her heart. We had just finished dinner and were walking down the street together toward the car when Grace suddenly collapsed. I called 911 on my cell and held her, waiting for the ambulance to arrive. I thought she was all ready gone until she opened her eyes suddenly and smiled at me."

"Sam." Shelby reached across the table to him, but he sat with his hands covering his face. When he finally took them down, his face was scarlet red. It appeared that only his sheer will was holding back the tears. Maybe that is why Sam got so mad at her. Anger was preferable to the sting of her death.

"You're still mourning for Grace and I'm…"

Shelby looked down at Ian's ring on her finger, "...standing headlong in the path of a F 5 tornado. I need your help. That's why I'm here."

"You don't have to do this alone anymore. You've got me now." Sam stood to his feet. "Right now, Noah and I better get going but I'll give you a call soon." Sam knelt on the living room floor beside his son, nudging him wake. "Hey, partner, time to get going. Need a lift?"

"No, I can walk," Noah answered, still half unconscious.

"That's my boy."

Shelby watched Sam and Noah walk hand in hand out the door. She went to her room and laid back into the deep embrace of her bed. *He's still in love with his wife.*

Shelby woke up at the sound of the ringing phone. She sat up. "Hello?"

A voice said, "Bonjour, Ivy..."

"Ian?" She must have been dreaming. Had to be dreaming because she couldn't have heard Ian. Could she?

Chapter Fourteen

She parked the car near a footpath. The incline was easy enough making the trail an easy go. The soil had a dark rich tone, like fresh ground coffee, only it smelled musty.

The path was well worn so she was fairly well assured she'd be meeting other hikers along her way and was surprised when she didn't. Sunlight filtered through the trees spreading a rich pattern across the leaf-littered ground. Although it was a sunny day, the area she hiked was often dark from all the foliage still precariously clinging to trees branches.

An early frost had already started the change of the leaves' colors. The wind caused some of them to lose their hold and float gently to the ground where the gold, red, orange and yellow crunched beneath the heavy step of her boot.

Shelby ducked beneath a few limbs along her way. Finally, she reached the first plateau where she decided to rest before heading back down again. By now it was late afternoon and she wanted to be at the base well before sunset. There was no way she was going to stumble around in the darkness up here, tripping over tree roots and making sure she wasn't going off the path.

Tugging off her boots, she sat beneath the heavy oak trees. Soon the sun dropped behind the horizon and the valley below was purple with something deeper than lavender. The goosebumps felt good along her arms. Pulling a sweater from the knapsack, she heard his voice as breaking waves behind her.

"Heureusement vous etes en bonne sante."

"Ian?"

"Oui; I'm here, Ivy."

His words caught in her heart. If she dared to look, would he be like the mountain fog that vanishes with the first touch of sunlight? Slowly, she got to her feet and turned around, hoping for the best, bracing for the worst.

Ian stood near the pine trees wearing jeans and a Yale sweatshirt with a plain cap. Pulling it off his head, she noticed that his hair was longer again. He looked fit and muscular and no longer wore glasses.

"It is you." Tears pearled at the corners of her eyes.

"Yes, it's me," he answered with that adorable inflection in his voice. Eyes and smile. How she had missed them.

Her hand fluttered to her heart. "You hung up the phone so quickly that I thought I had imagined it, but here you are."

"Me voici. And here you are."

"How is this possible? You're dead. I'm losing my mind, aren't I?" She ran her fingertips over her forehead. The mountain air was playing tricks on her mind. She closed her eyes and then opened them. He was still there.

"I was hit, but not as badly as it seemed. My bulletproof vest took the worst of it, but I sure got the wind knocked out of me."

"The agents outside my hospital room said you were dead," Shelby insisted as though trying to convince him.

"The bullets were removed and a few stitches later, I was headed out to find you. All within two hours."

"This is unbelievable." She wanted to dance,

yell, jump up and down but most of all she wanted to touch him. Yet she was afraid to move in case this was all a dream.

Ian held out his hand. She stood her ground for a moment longer and then ran to him. Shelby jumped into his arms and wrapped her legs around his waist. She touched his face, his hands. He grinned at her and she was safe again. Ian hugged her tightly and then set her down on the ground. Shelby kissed his cheek. He returned it on her cheek. She kissed his other cheek.

He stared into her eyes before lowering his gaze to her mouth. His lips descended slowly toward them while her heart stood still. When they finally touched, she responded with joyous relief as if a dam broke inside and burst over them as a waterfall. Then just as suddenly, Shelby shoved him away.

"What?"

"At least you could have told me you were still alive!" A fresh anger added itself to Shelby's emotional state.

He drew in a long breath, savoring the moment. "I couldn't." He wrapped both arms around her and pulled her into him. Their kisses grew increasingly intense, as their bodies began to rock together in rhythm. She felt the ring on her finger. Ian had a wife. Ian was married. Shelby shoved him away.

"What?"

"Your wife, that's what! I've been feeling so sad for your wife and now that you're not dead, I'm making love to her husband. Your children must hate me!"

He drew in a long breath, "I'm not married."

"Oh yes, you are; I have your wedding ring to prove it!" She held it out.

"I never said it was my wedding ring. I've never been married; never had time for it," he answered bluntly and held her gaze.

"Really? Are you sure?" She tipped her head to one side.

"Yes, quite sure. I, of all people, would know this," he said as Shelby felt his breath on her face. She smelled peppermint. His voice was soft and deep. She was lost in his scent, his sound, his gaze.

"Let's get back to how glad you are I'm alive." He pulled his long fingers through her dark hair and directed her head to his mouth in order to kiss her lips again. Passion returned more intensely this time. Her cheeks felt flush from the touch of Ian's fabulous lips. He sure knew how to use them. If he is half as good with his gun aim as he was with his lips, she was sure he was an expert marksman

"About a hundred times I thought about the moment you would find out I wasn't dead and not once did I imagine this kind of reception," Ian said joyously. "I must admit it beats to pieces what I had pictured."

"Am I being too forward?" Shelby withdrew.

"No, I rather like it." He pulled her to him. "When you cross the line of my sense of morality, I'll stop you."

"Suddenly, I'm filled with such hope. Ian, our road together has been long and difficult. Yet…now…here you are…and here I am."

But, where is my brain? Tears splashed down her cheeks. Stomping her foot in frustration, she took hold of Ian again, kissing him hard. All thoughts of everything unrelated to Ian swam right out of her head. His hands slowly moved down to her spine as chills whooshed over her.

Everything was happening so fast. Shelby found that she couldn't think straight and pulled back slightly from Ian. "Ian, please…"

"Please what, darlin', I'm right here. Just hold on tight."

"So much has happened. I still can't believe

you're here. My heart broke when I thought I had lost you."

He slowly lowered his lips to hers and just before they touched, he whispered, "You have no idea how hard it has been to stay away."

She breathlessly pulled away and rubbed her hand across her face. "We've got to stop this. We need to talk." Ian's kisses felt good, perhaps a little too good.

"This is way more fun than talking." He looked into her eyes. "Your eyes are flecked with gold and your skin is so fair; I bet you could even burn in sixty-degree weather. Look, the sun leaves behind little freckles on your skin." He touched first her arm, then her cheek as his fingertips followed the trail of freckles. Shelby had never felt this way before.

"C'mon, let's sit over under those trees for awhile." He invited her with a smile as he picked up her boots, put her canteen back in her knapsack and walked off with them. Shelby knew she had to follow. There was no choice. "C'mon" seemed like a powerful word to her.

Like a lamb being led, Shelby followed Ian willingly until something prickly dug in her heel. "Ow." She grabbed her foot.

Ian was quick to return to her side, kneeling in front of her. "Looks like a burr to me," Ian said examining her foot.

"It really hurts."

"Sit on this log and I'll pull the nasty thing out."

Shelby plopped down. Ian took a hold of it and yanked it straight out. "How's that?" He kissed her toes.

"So much better," she gasped.

Ian shoved her boots into the knapsack and hooked the straps over her shoulders. Then he picked Shelby up and carried her over his shoulder toward the shade under an oak that had to have been there for a hundred years. Ian stopped, looked around and obviously felt the place was secluded enough because he set her gently back down on the ground. He dropped the knapsack and sank down beside her.

"It's not anyplace fancy but at least we're alone," his voice was gravely with emotion as she looked up into his eyes.

He gently touched her cheek, "I have thought of you so much and had so many things I wanted to say to you. Sitting here now, I can't think of any of them. All I want to do is be with you." He again touched his lips to hers. The heart rate that had begun to slow now changed its tune.

As his hand began to trail up her back, she couldn't help but stiffen a bit. He must have felt it too because he pulled back. She could see the question in his eyes.

"Ian, I've never…well…been with a man." She reached for him again, as he retreated from her a bit more. "Please…with you…I feel things I've never felt before and they scare me."

His voice was softer now and he reached for her hand. "I'm glad you told me. This started out as a quick romp in the woods but then it turned into something much better. Your first time will be our first time together, and it's not going to be in the woods with sticks poking us in our backside."

If she wasn't almost in love with him, this would have been the clincher. "Ian, this may seem silly but I feel like you are an answer to my prayers."

He had to chuckle a bit at that. "An answer to prayers? Humm, I've been called a lot of things but never that."

They reached for one another again and Shelby felt herself land in Ian's embrace. It was a calm, restful place. They sat underneath the pines with their arms wrapped around each other. Shelby listened to Ian's heart pounding in his chest. She had a volatile mix of feelings and emotions running through her. "I need answers, Ian."

"Like what?" he asked gently and kissed her forehead.

"Why did those men think you were dead?" Shelby had to know.

"I wanted it that way. It'd stop them from trying to kill me again," Ian chuckled.

"Who were they?"

"That's still in discovery. Next question."

"Where have you been all this time?" She longed to have the answer.

"You mean after I fixed the hospital alarm and got those two thug agents away from you?"

"That was you?" Shelby asked with surprise.

"And since then I've been to Austin, Oklahoma, Colorado, Arizona."

"But that's where I've been." She looked into his eyes quizzically.

"I told you that you're under my jurisdiction and that I would always protect you. I also came to the hospital when you had the asthma attack." Ian pulled his ring from Shelby's finger. Then he took out a pocketknife and with the edge of it, popped off the stone.

"What are you doing?" Shelby protested, not wanting him to destroy the ring.

"Inside is a transmitter that let me keep track of you within a fifty mile radius."

"I thought you said the ring was passed down through generations."

"Yup, it was...passed down from generations of spies."

"That's deceitful! I loved that ring. It was a symbol of courage for me."

"It seems to me it worked."

“I mourned for you with that ring and for you it was nothing more—”

“It was a way to find you. The ruby isn’t the jewel. The real jewel is you.” Ian took her by the hand. “You came to the foothills for answers.”

“I came here to—”

“Find answers.” Ian tucked a piece of her hair behind her ear.

“And you found me…” Overcome by emotions, words strangled in her throat.

“The way you handled yourself was truly amazing. My own trained agents couldn’t have done me prouder. By the way, I like what you’ve done with your hair.” He gently tugged a clump. All of Ian’s touches were welcome.

“Why didn’t you let me know you were close? I would’ve been less afraid.”

“My sweet lady, I was everywhere you looked including the cabbie who took you to and from the cemetery and helped you with your mail drop.”

“Are you kidding me?”

“Nope. I never kid and that’s an important fact you need to keep in mind about me. It was hard staying in the background and away from you. I didn’t need to complicate the relationship. Besides I have my own troop of ‘unfriendlies’ looking for me as well. If they find me, I don’t want to lead them right to you.”

“Don’t tell me you were on the same bus I took?”

“No, I wasn’t, but I was in the car behind the bus.” Ian looked up at the sky. “It’s late, I better get going.” He put the ring back together and handed it to Shelby. Ian moved toward a trail.

“Wait! You can’t just walk away and leave me here!” Shelby’s voice shook with feeling. “Ian, I’ve really missed you.”

Ian started back toward her. She got up and ran to him with her heart open wide. When she fell into his arms, Ian dipped his head into the hollow of her throat and his lips touched her skin. She loved the way he made her feel.

"There's so much more to say. I did what you told me to do, to sleep with my hands ready and to think with my head, not my emotions."

"Good, that's my girl." He slid the back of his hand along the side of her face. "Get your boots on and I'll walk you to the trail."

Shelby wiggled her feet back into the boots and Ian knelt down to tie them. They walked for a short distance in silence. When they reached the fork in the pathway, she tugged on his arm. "Please stay with me. I don't want to be away from you again."

"My darling, I've never been far."

"But I don't know that. We need a sign, so I'll know you're somewhere close."

Ian thought for a moment. "What's your favorite flower?"

"Viola Sorbet Yesterday, Today and Tomorrow," she blurted.

"Oh." He seemed disappointed.

"What's wrong?"

"For some reason I figured you for a daisy kind of girl." Ian scratched the back of his head.

"Then you figured wrong."

"I've never heard of that Viola kind before today." He looked perplexed.

"The flowers are dainty, and when their blooms open, they're white. Gradually they turn to shades of blue."

"I was hoping for something more on the ordinary side, something easy to find."

"Gotcha. How about daisies then? You can find them in any supermarket, any time of the year."

"Good choice and it sounds a bit like me." He laughed and then touched the end of her nose. "Now close your eyes and make a wish."

"What kind of a wish?" Shelby tilted her head to the side.

"A beautiful wish but you have to close your eyes first."

"All right, my eyes are officially closed now."

"Of all the people in the world, who do you wish to see more than anyone else, other than me?" He whispered in her ear."

His breath tickled. Then she latched onto her wish and tears welled and seeped from her eyelids. "My parents!" Shelby blurted. "I haven't seen them or heard their voice for over a year. I've always been so close to them."

Ian held Shelby as she cried into his chest. "I am used to being on my own without any personal entanglements, but you're not made that way. I forgot that; I'm sorry."

"Ian, make this all go away so I can go home. There was a time I wanted to run away from Twin Lakes and never go back. Now all I want to do is go home." She took a step back. Looking up at him, she blinked back tears. "Can you do that? Take me home?"

"Come on, it's late and night falls quickly in the mountains. By the way, I have something for you." He reached down inside his pocket and withdrew a small object, then tossed it to her. It was her inhaler. She wrapped her fingers around it.

"When will I see you again?"

"Soon," he promised. "Way before that one runs out."

"Ian, don't leave me. Not just yet." Her voice broke. "Stay a little longer?"

He pressed his hand against her face. "I'm never far from you."

Shelby watched as he disappeared into the woods just as a couple of hikers passed. Reluctantly, she followed the path back down toward the parking lot where her car waited. Feeling light as air, she touched things along the way; the bark on trees, rocks, low branches—as though they could hold her down to earth all because Ian was alive and love had prevailed.

Chapter Fifteen

Shelby wasn't one for reruns. Watching any movie or TV show one time was plenty for her. However, images of Ian were altogether different. He was a genre all on his own. Her mind kept pushing the replay button of their afternoon spent together and she relished each moment. The spontaneous rendezvous was a week ago. It was time for the sequel.

Filled with energy and needing a distraction, Shelby took a long walk around the town park and then stopped to admire the new seasonal dresses in the window displays of Barton's Department Store. One caught her eye; it was beyond cute. Shelby sighed. It was a frivolous expense since she didn't need it. Winter sweaters were a much more practical purchase.

She had only been gone an hour by the time she arrived back at her cottage. Automatically, she checked her mailbox on the way up the walk. Utility bills were all that ever came if you didn't count the occasional envelope filled with coupons.

When she opened the mailbox today, a surprise waited for her. A small bouquet of daisies lay on top of a folded piece of paper.

"Ian," she smiled, holding them up to her nose to catch their sweet scent. Then, as she ran the soft petals over her cheek, she remembered. He was near. With her heart racing, Shelby darted back down the walkway and pushed open the gate. She looked up and down the block, praying to catch sight of him but she was let down.

Anxious as she was to read the note, standing out on the sidewalk certainly wasn't the place. She'd read it alone in the perfect privacy of her garden. Shelby held the daisies to her nose again as she walked around the side of the house. She sat down on the iron bench and for a moment held the message to her breast, imagining endearing phrases penned by Ian's own hand. Surely, he poured his heart out in it. She looked at the note again, unfolded it and read.

In two days at noon.

1223 Washington Ave.

East side entrance.

Charleston, West Virginia.

Shelby read it again, feeling certain there must be something she was missing. Disappointment sunk deep over the lack of meaningful prose until she realized this must be the address of their next rendezvous.

It was the time to prepare for the tryst. There were only two days until she was in Ian's arms again. It had been so long since she had been on a date that she hoped she remembered how to get ready for one. Shelby stood in front of her closet. Everything she wore had been from the time she spent in Austin. Then she remembered the dress in the store window. Perfect.

Shelby got her purse and went back to town to buy the dress. She picked out shoes and jewelry to match. This was fun. On the way home, she filled up the car with gas. A full tank was always a good thing when you were on your way to meet your love. In the evening, Shelby charted her route to Charleston on the Internet and printed out her turn-by-turn map. She had to be on time.

The night before she was to meet Ian was spent sleeplessly. She was bursting at the seams to share her joy with someone and Jerrica was the perfect candidate. However, that was impossible. If she explained Ian, then she would have to explain the trouble she was in and who she really was. None of that could happen.

When the day arrived, Shelby was up early. She hummed away as she showered, shaved, powdered, combed, perfumed, twisted her hair into a French knot and shimmied into her dress. The jewelry was the added touch. After she slipped into her new pumps, she stepped in front of the full-length mirror to get the effect.

Shelby gasped. The hair on her head looked like a round burl of a seaweed clump and the dress didn't look anywhere near as nice on her as it had at the store. In fact it looked like a pattern that should be on a dinner plate. She was a walking sideshow. What had she done? This whole getup just wasn't her style. Shelby returned to the bathroom, washed her face, brushed out her hair, removed her jewelry and changed her clothes.

Her next visit to the mirror showed jeans with a long sleeved shirt and a jacket. The new shoes worked with the outfit so they could stay. The dress would be returned to the store tomorrow. Shelby was out the door heading for Charleston just after dawn.

Right on time, she drove into the city limits and with her directions easily located the address. When Shelby saw the building, she knew it had to be wrong so she double-checked the note and read the numbers above the church door. This couldn't be right; it just couldn't. Shelby got out of the car and walked up to the front door of the church. She figured she was now facing north so she followed the sidewalk around to the side of the building. There was the door on the east side. According to Ian's note, it was going to be open.

Shelby stood in front of the entry wondering if

she should turn the knob and walk inside. Suddenly, she felt frightened. There was no guarantee that Ian had actually written the note; to be honest, she had never seen his handwriting so she wouldn't really know if it was his. Her curiosity got the best of her. She turned the knob, pushed open the door and entered, stepping into a narrow unlit corridor. At the end was a light coming from a room. She heard voices. Shelby took a step and then another. She kept walking, listening to the sound of her new shoes hitting against the floor, touching the clammy stonewalls with her hands.

The area opened into a large square room with period couches from the nineteenth century. Sunlight streamed through the south facing windows. Along the walls were hung dozens of pictures framed in gesso. An elderly couple was studying one of them on the far wall. The man's head looked like a q-tip and the woman was far too thin. Shelby's heart quickened. She felt compelled to walk toward them.

"Paul," the older woman spoke. "I like this one the best. See how the artist used light for the sinner to find his way to God."

The man nodded in agreement. "I think it's my favorite out of the ones we've seen so far this morning, Rita."

"Mom? Dad? Is that really you?" Shelby gasped.

The couple immediately turned. Rita seized her husband's arm. "Ivy!"

****

By the time Shelby returned to her cottage, a half moon was rising. She kept all the lights in the house off and sat in her yard remembering the day.

Then from the stillness of the night he came. "Was it a good day for you, Shelby?"

He stood in foxgloves now dead from frost. "You've never called me by that name before."

"No wonder you get lonely. Fine parents have raised you. I like them."

Shelby rushed into his arms. "How were you able to arrange it?"

"Easy." Ian rocked back on his heels, almost being toppled over as she lunged at him. "Your parents were the recipients of a sweepstakes. They had twenty-four hours to pack before the limousine arrived to take them to the airport where they flew to West Virginia. They were provided a three night stay at a five star hotel with an itinerary made out for them. All they had to do was follow it and the second stop today was Saint Joseph's Cathedral where valuable paintings from the Renaissance period were on display for a limited time. Only it was a private showing…just for them. Just for you."

"You thought of everything. Ian, I will forever adore you for this." She saw a sparkle in his eyes. Was she the reason for the happiness she saw in them?

"I like the sound of those words. Say more…" Ian hooked a piece of hair behind one ear and kissed the top of her head.

"I will. Take a seat." She motioned toward an iron chair. "We have all night to talk."

Chapter Sixteen

In front of her was the most exquisite bouquet of daisies. Shelby found a bunch of them tied into a fancy bouquet on the steps of her porch. It was evident Ian had to have gone to a nursery to find them. These weren't the run of the mill daisies but painted daisies with blue centers. The image of him walking up and down the aisles to select these particular daisies was intoxicating. It took time to do this. Shelby looked for a note but there wasn't any, not this time. Three days had passed since the last time they were together and Ian was all she could think about. The tenor of Ian's voice was soft and low, becoming the music of her heart. Ian was the hero of her love story, balancer of her idiocy, the focus of her daydreams.

At night she stood at the windows hoping for a glimpse of him. Every little noise in the cottage, made her think Ian was coming. For a time she even sat in the garden replaying the night they talked to dawn, hoping to see Ian magically reappear. A year ago she was so focused on work and finding a career, and now, all that energy seemed to be put into thoughts of Ian. What she needed was a diversion. Baking apple pies just wasn't it. Just as she took the third pie from the oven and set them on the counter to cool, the doorbell rang. "Ian!" Shelby sprinted through the kitchen, down the hall and flung open the front door.

"What's this all about?" Shelby looked into the faces of Noah and Sam. She masked her disappointment with a smile.

"I have a puppy!" Noah yelped. "Do you see him, Ms. Shelby? I told you Jesus would get me one but Daddy beat him to it."

The puppy jerked, twisted and whined, demanding to be put down on the floor. By the look on his face, Sam was definitely enthusiastic about the purchase.

"We've had it just two days and the dog is already spoiled rotten."

The puppy paused to smell Shelby's feet at the same time a yellow puddle spread across her freshly cleaned linoleum floor.

"Oh no." Sam snatched a wad of paper towels and wiped it up as Shelby smiled a little too broadly for sincerity purposes. She rubbed the Bernese Mountain dog's neck and ears. "You're a cute thing. Sam, she's already pretty big and look at the size of those paws! Just how big will it be when fully grown?"

"Not big; about the size of a Saint Bernard."

"That's huge!"

"Nah, that's not huge. A pony or a horse is big. An elephant is what's huge," Sam corrected. "I think I better set this little gal out on the patio for the time being, okay?" He opened the French door and out ran the puppy, followed by Noah.

Before Sam's posterior hit the seat of the chair, Shelby had plunked down a warm piece of apple pie and a fork right in front of him. "I'll have you know that this is my Mother's prize winning recipe. She won First Place at the State Fair three years in a row!"

He opened his mouth wide, taking a big bite. "Mmmm, I've never tasted better!" With a mouth filled with pie, a trickle of warm syrup squeezed from between his lips and dripped down on his shirt as he dipped his fork back into the fruit.

"Here, let me help. That stain will set if we don't take care of it right away." Shelby took a bit of soda water and vinegar and dabbed at his shirt with a sponge. She could feel Sam staring at her as she kept hers fastened to the stain. *If you have feelings for me, Sam Oliver, all I can say is this is really bad timing.*

"Ivy, I have news." He stopped her hands.

She glanced about to see if Noah had heard her real name but he was still outside. "What?"

"It's not the kind of news we wanted to hear. I did some checking and rechecking on your FBI Agent Ian Serby."

She felt herself warm at the sound of Ian's name and prayed she wasn't blushing. Sam was too good of a reporter for her to give too much away.

"No agent by that name was killed."

She knew that all ready. For the moment, she'd play along. "Then what I heard about his death was wrong. That's good to know. Phew, a total relief! Thanks for the news, Sam. More pie?" She immediately started slicing another piece.

"No thanks." He placed his fork on his plate and slid it away from him, giving her his full attention. "In fact, there's no agent by that name in the bureau nor has there ever been anyone by that name since its inception."

"I don't understand." Shelby sat down.

"The men you were with the night of the car attack are a team of maverick agents who operate within the system called Wildcards. The FBI believes you were planted at the White House by them."

She had spent a delightful afternoon with a Wildcard, a maverick agent. What a desperate woman she had become. Shelby bit her lip to keep from crying.

"There's something different about you," Sam

noticed.

"What?" Shelby turned her head not wanting Sam to read her thoughts.

"I have more bad news. I'm not sure how to tell you this so will just say it straight out. Ivy Elizabeth Dillon, you are number five on the FBI Most Wanted list with a million dollar reward."

"I don't believe it!" She snapped.

"Go see for yourself on the Internet news."

Shelby pushed back from the table and sat down at her computer in the living room. It was just as Sam had said. There it was—a picture of her face with her name beneath it. WANTED: Ivy Elizabeth Dillon. It was a picture of her with red hair and freckles that showed up as lop-sided splotches. It wasn't a flattering image in the least. The only good thing was that her present disguise was believable after all. Right now that was little comfort. Shelby pressed print and put it on top of her pile of papers and closed the folder.

"Sam, I wasn't even in Washington at the time Ms Waters was murdered. I was in Chicago. Rob Gram or Erin will vouch for me; pick up that phone and call them!" She hurried back into the kitchen and pointed at the pink wall phone. Through tears she demanded, "Call!"

"Are you sure you and Erin didn't take a quick trip into D.C., say for a day?" He raised his eyebrows.

She felt like melting ice cream. "Oh, I forgot. Yes, we did. Our Washington apartment had been broken into months before and the police notified us our stolen goods were found. We had to identify them."

"The plane reservation is in your name plus cell phone records of calling Ms. Waters' personal line on the day she went missing have all been verified. I listened to your voice message saying you had to see her. Ms. Waters told the Vice President she was meeting you for lunch."

"And you can't have a better witness than that."

"You inhaler was found in the pocket of her jacket when her body washed up on shore."

"Sam, I lose my inhalers all the time," Shelby protested.

"And there is your DNA under her fingernails."

"That is a flat out manufacturing of evidence. Sam, I told you, Erin *and* I went to D.C. just to identify our stolen items. I called Ms. Waters to invite her for lunch but there was no answer. Yes, I left that message on her voice mail but I never saw her or got a call back. Erin will back me up; she was with me the entire time."

"Well, she's not backing you up." Sam stared into her eyes.

"What? You talked to her?"

"The Bureau talked to her. I read their report."

"And?"

"Erin told officials she had to identify the stolen goods alone because you had a meeting with someone whose name you refused to disclose to her."

"She's a liar!" Shelby screamed as she hit the table with her fists. "Why is she saying that? Wait! The police department will have a record that we were both there identifying our stuff. We had to sign in and out."

"I've already thought of that and personally went to the precinct to have a look at the books. They show only *her* signature."

"This is crazy! I must be a very dangerous person for all this cover-up work." Shelby spun around and began pacing the room. "Someone must have threatened Erin for her to lie like this. For a while she had to live under an assumed name and now I am doing the same thing. Don't you find this a bit too coincidental?"

Sam got to his feet to grab her hands. He held them together in his. "Sweetie, I wish I could make things better for you."

"Could Erin be getting back at me for her sister's death?"

"Why would she even want to do that? It makes no sense at all."

Shelby typed Twin Lakes Newspaper into the browser and went to the archive page. "Back in Chicago, we had a discussion about where Karin's body was found. I said it was found a long way from the club, over on the Illinois side of the lake."

"I remember."

"Erin said Karin was found by the Yacht Club." In the archives, Shelby looked for the year of Karin's death. Finally, the article came up and Shelby pointed at the screen. "There it is, Sam. Karin was found where I remembered."

"I don't understand what this has to do with now?" Sam shook his head.

"I don't either but somehow it does. Are you still willing to help me?"

"Yes, of course! I'll always help you, Ivy."

"Sam, you better remember to call me Shelby, just in case, so you don't slip up when it really matters," she whispered, remembering how Erin had given her the same talk about calling her Jordan.

Interrupting, Noah suddenly ran in from playing with his pup. "I thought of a name for my pup-pee."

Shelby turned her head so he wouldn't see her so upset and become frightened.

"Great, what did you name her?" Sam quietly asked.

"Flower. Ms. Shelby has so many of them out here and she likes rolling in them and eating them. She chewed up lots of them. See some sticking out the sides of her mouth?" He pointed outside toward the dog wildly swinging her tongue about her nose in an attempt to swallow the long stems.

"Ah no, Noah!" Sam started toward the back door.

"Wait, let them play and have fun, Sam. It's all right. Sit here with me and please don't leave," Shelby begged.

"I'll stay." Turning back to his son, Sam said, "Noah, go ahead and play some more in the garden with Flower."

When Noah was out of earshot, Shelby said, "I need to tell you something, Sam. Last week when I hiked into the Blue Ridge foothills, I saw the man who I know as Ian Serby."

"You told me he was dead." Sam looked suspicious.

Shelby had to keep his faith in her. "I wouldn't lie to you. He was shot right in front of me and the agents said he was dead. Evidently, he faked his death. He's the one who disarmed the security alarm at the hospital."

"I'd like to know his motive but my bet is that he did it to get you out on the street where the Wildcards could take care of you."

The vase of daisies on the kitchen table caught her eye. Maybe like the ring, they were bugged, too. Shelby crossed to the kitchen, shoved them down into the garbage and then took the bag out. When she walked back in, she leaned against the counter, trying to figure out what to say next.

"He told me about there being two parts to the FBI—the good and the bad. He said somewhat the same as what you told me today, but he didn't have a name for the other unit. He said he was part of the good unit." She had one thing left worth telling and that was about seeing her parents. She couldn't tell Sam about Ian's passionate kisses and the fact she was falling for a man she didn't understand. She couldn't bear to talk about it.

No way would she tell Sam she made a fool of herself time and time again with this man, and not only put herself into jeopardy but her parents as well. If spies traded stories, and she imagined they might, then this so called Ian Serby could be laughing his head off right this moment to his fellow spies'. *Wait, that is only if he isn't telling me the truth. How could someone be so sweet to her and yet be so false? Maybe he is part of the good unit.*

"Shelby, from now on you need to be totally invisible and let me work this investigation. Since I'm a political news anchor, I won't raise suspicion. It's my job."

"Sam, I can't just sit here and do nothing."

"Ian knows you are staying here, right?"

She nodded.

"That worries me." Sam paced the floor for a few minutes. "Do you have electrical timers for lamps?"

"There were some here when I moved in."

Sam began opening cabinets and peering inside closets. As if another thought suddenly hit him, he looked out each window and then pulled the shades closed all through the house. He went to the door to check on his son. "Noah!" he called. "I want you and…what did you say the pup's name is now?"

"*Buddy*. It's Buddy!"

"Okay, you and Buddy come up and stay right here on the summer porch, do you understand me? Don't go down into the yard anymore; it's getting dark."

"Yes, Dad." Noah took Buddy by the collar and pulled her along. When they were inside, Sam closed and locked the porch doors. He paused at the windows to look out.

"Here." Shelby nudged Sam, handing him the timers she found in the kitchen drawers. "What do you need with these anyway?" She had to admit that all of his actions were making her a bit nervous.

"I'm plugging lamps into them. Then I'll set the timer so they will go on and off at the predetermined time. It'll give the illusion of you being here even though you won't be. Pack a small bag but don't tidy up anything. I want the inside of the cottage to appear as though you're still staying here."

"What about Jerrica? We talk every day and I pay her rent the first of each month. She will call the police if I suddenly disappear."

"Good point. I'll come up with some story that you had to leave for a short while and I'll pay your rent in the meantime."

"Stop right there." Shelby glared at him. "I have my own money and can pay the rent myself."

"Eventually, I'll tell her you left for good." Sam ignored her offer.

Shelby sighed. After years of being out of her life, he was certainly making up for lost time, trampling back in and taking over. But maybe there was a reason for this. A million dollars was a lot of money. She watched him suspiciously as he began hooking lamps up to the timers, setting them to turn on by five that evening and off by midnight but setting each one just a few minutes off the other. He did the TV as well setting it to his news station. "I'm moving your car around to the back of the house and driving my truck into the garage so no one will see you leave with me. Stay down on the floorboards when we pull out; keep low till I tell you differently."

"Where are you taking me?" Shelby felt frightened over the possibilities.

"I'm remodeling a barn into a house. There's a secret room at the top peak under the eaves beneath the roofline that you can live in for now. It's perfect since it has no windows and you'll be able to use the lights. Even has a private bath. I have a small refrigerator in my garage that I'll move up there for you and the microwave from the kitchen."

"Oh, no! This is not Nazi Germany! I refuse to go into hiding like this. Besides you know how claustrophobic I can get." Shelby nearly screamed at him.

"Let me explain something to you about your situation…any minute now either an assassin or the FBI could come through your front door. Either scenario is bad for you. This Ian Serby may have his own personal agenda and is keeping tabs on you. Shelby, those are three good reasons why you have to go into hiding. Something tells me he is watching the house and I want him to think you're still here at least for a few days. These timers will create that illusion."

"Sam, how do I know I can trust you?" Her voice was sharper than she meant it.

"What are you inferring?" Sam narrowed his gaze at her angrily.

"You expect me to go blindly with you out into the night and squirrel up in a corner of your so called attic."

"I want you to be safe."

"How can I be sure you're not turning me in for the reward?"

The words kicked the wind out of him. Sam's face crumbled into a look of betrayal. "Is that what you really think? If that was going to happen, I would have had the FBI pick you up at the hospital."

"Sorry, Sam. I feel ashamed of myself."

"Good, you should."

"Maybe it'd be best for me to meet Ian again so I can find out who he really is. What do you think, huh?" She gripped Sam's arm.

"No, you are not meeting with this crackpot again. It's too dangerous. We're doing it my way from here on out."

She nodded and released her hold on Sam.

Shelby was sure her way was the best, but for now it was better if Sam thought she was going along with his plan.

"Go pack. I'll bring the truck into the garage." Sam stopped in his tracks. "Wait, I forgot about Noah. Maybe I can take him to his babysitter, Betty Lou. The trailer park isn't far from here so I'll drop him off and then come back for you. It's best he doesn't know you'll be at the barn; being so young he might slip. I don't want him in the middle of this. See ya in ten minutes. Be ready." He held up his finger to her as if he were a hall monitor in school.

Sam would be back soon. She had to act fast. As a refugee fleeing an approaching army would, Shelby ran into the bedroom and threw all her disguises into one suitcase and shut the lid. Sam wasn't allowed to know about them. He'd figure she'd go out wearing one and he'd be right. Into the second suitcase, she put clothes and cosmetics, soap, shampoo. She loved this little cottage with its garden. How she hated to trade it for a windowless room without sky.

The sound of a shrill ring against the dead silence made her jump. She looked at it for a few rings before picking it up. Only Jerrica called her and now Sam. Picking up the small cordless, it read as an anonymous number.

"Yes?" she answered in a whisper.

"Bonjour."

"Ian." No matter what Sam told her about him, Ian still buckled her knees. "I got your bouquet."

"I know."

"They're beautiful."

"Like you."

She laughed uncomfortably.

"I watched you when you discovered them. You looked around for me."

"I would have preferred you delivering them in

person?"

Ian chuckled. "That is exactly what I wanted to do."

Shelby worried Ian would see Sam at her place. "And where are you now?" She picked up the corner of the curtain and looked up and down the block, praying he wasn't close.

"I had to go to Washington today to check out a few leads. Shelby, this case has gotten to me. I find I am focusing on us instead of this case. You're in my mind. I want us to be together, always."

Her heart stopped for a moment as her edgy nerves began to pick along her hairline in the form of perspiration. "Ian, who am I hiding from?"

"Wildcards."

Shelby hoped Sam would take his time in returning. "Tell me, are you part of them?"

"No, I'm not."

"I'm glad. Ian, I want to trust you." Shelby meant it. She had feelings for him. Lots and lots of feelings for him. "When can I see you again?"

"Tomorrow."

"Where should we meet?" She could see Sam's truck at the stop sign. Shelby had to get off the phone fast.

"There's a park in Richmond on Gettysburg Avenue. Do you know where it's at?"

"I'll Google it."

"I'll be on a bench near the statue of Grant facing west."

"What time?"

"Eleven a.m."

Sam pulled his truck into her garage.

"That's perfect."

"You're perfect."

"I'm not."

"You're perfect for me."

She heard the truck's door slam.

"We need to talk."

The back door squeaked opened, then slammed shut.

"Yes, we do."

Footsteps came down the hall.

"See you then. Just don't ever lie to me." She told him and set the phone down.

"Who was that?"

Shelby jumped and turned around to see Sam standing in the doorway. "A telemarketer."

Sam narrowed his gaze at her.

"I warned them not to lie to me anymore...or, I'll insist they remove my name from their call list."

Sam picked up her luggage. "Come on, the sooner we leave the better it'll be for both of us."

Shelby looked down at Ian's ring. She had to make a split second decision what to do with it. Keeping it with her would serve as a beacon and lead Ian straight to Sam's door. Sam didn't trust Ian, and at the moment, Shelby wasn't sure if she did. Not anymore. For that matter, she wasn't altogether sure if Sam was all that trustworthy himself. In that scenario, it might be good to have the ring with her.

"Shelby!"

Quickly, she slid the ring off her finger, dropped it into a drawer and closed it. She had made her decision and prayed it was the right one.

Chapter Seventeen

Sam punched in the numbers on the alarm panel.

He had said he was turning a barn into a house but it sure appeared that the work was pretty close to done. Whitewashed pine floors ran the length of the first floor and the walls were still raw plasterboard. Down the hall was a kitchen complete with new unstained built-ins and a cozy connecting family room with a brick fireplace in the far corner. There was an open balcony on the second floor closed in with an iron grate.

"Follow me," Sam instructed, pushing aside a panel revealing a hidden staircase.

"Pretty cool. So gothic." Shelby followed Sam up the steps. At the top was a small landing with a doorway leading into a small bedroom.

"Here's your room." Sam set her luggage on the floor. A twin bed was pushed against the wall. A bare bulb hung from the ceiling. She could see into the private bath from where she stood. There was no towel on the rack.

"Cozy. Just about the size of a coffin."

"Nice to find you so grateful."

"Sorry." Being claustrophobic, Shelby closed her eyes willing away a full blown panic attack. She breathed deeply. The barn had all the smells of a new house with freshly sawn wood and sawdust. Not good for asthma. She hoped she had enough medicine left in her inhaler. Oh, that's right, Ian brought her a new one. But where was it anyway?

She remembered now, it was in her knapsack at home with the book on Ancient Egypt. Double darn!

"I'm leaving my cell phone here with you in case you need to get a hold of me. Here are the numbers where I can be reached. If you need to leave a message just say 'Shelby called'. When I call back, I'll let it ring three times and then will call again. Answer it, but don't say anything till you hear my voice. Okay?"

"Okay."

"Let me show you the house alarm and explain how to use it with the code. The alarm will alert you to an intruder. If you are safe upstairs in your nest, just stay put. If the alarm goes off and you can't make it up here, then get out of the house as fast as you can."

Within minutes, Sam's cell phone rang. On the other end was his producer with an emergency at the station. Sam stewed, "Look, I'd love to stay longer but now I've got to be in Washington. I'll call Betty Lou and tell her I'm on my way to pick up Noah. His nanny is at the townhouse. I'll drop him there on the way to the studio." Sam punched in the numbers on his cell phone and began pacing. Shelby could tell from the tone of his voice and his curt way of speaking that Betty Lou irritated him. Sam kissed Shelby's cheek and then hurried out the back door.

Alone in the darkness of the house, Shelby peeked outside watching Sam drive down the driveway. He turned left heading north toward Washington.

Hungry, Shelby scrounged about in the refrigerator. All she found were a half eaten apple with Noah's teeth prints, sour milk, some awful chili fixings with a twinge of green mold, and a loaf of bread that was more like a brick. *Gotta stock this or I'll starve to death! What was Sam thinking? I'll visit a grocery store way out of town on my way back from meeting Ian tomorrow.*

Shelby went up the stairs to bed trying to figure out Ian's intentions. Why did this man pull on her heartstrings so? She tried to be logical in the way she was thinking. Sam was back in her life now. She knew Sam—his strengths and his weaknesses. Things might not have gone well the first time but it might be possible to have him for good this second time around.

But, she wasn't so sure she wanted that anymore. Changes had taken place since Sam broke their engagement back in Twin Lakes. He left a girl who regarded him as her entire universe. Now she was a woman with a mind of her own.

Then there was Ian. Yes, she knew Sam but it was Ian who made her heart race. She could try to talk herself into Sam all day but her heart wasn't listening.

The darkness at the top of the stairs was thick and frightening especially when combined with the way her mind was currently working. She snapped on the overhead light. Shelby washed her face, brushed her teeth, and got into her nightgown. It was an eerie feeling being in a new place by alone. The old barn had creaks and noises all its own. She might not be afraid of the dark any longer, but before Shelby went to sleep, she turned on the bathroom light and left the door ajar.

As she settled down into the bed, she sighed. "Please let me sleep tonight. I don't want to think any longer. It wears me out."

****

The next morning, Shelby put together an old lady outfit on the fly for today's outing. Modifying the outfit a bit she slid into an old coat she found in the barn's downstairs closet. It was black and hung long on her, nearly to her ankles. Her hair was all gray now thanks to her morning rinse and she pulled a scarf over her hair, tying it beneath her chin. She wore matron's shoes with thick heels and rolled up beige nylons. With lots of white pancake base on her face, accented with dark shadows in the hollows of her cheeks and beneath her eyes, she was really starting to look the part.

To complete the look, she walked bent over and carried a paper sack with handles she'd use to pick up park garbage. Not her usual date outfit. In her pocket, she tucked Sam's digital camera which she found while snooping about the place. A photo might be a good way to find out who Ian really was.

Sam had left his truck keys on the counter which wasn't particularly smart of Sam but helped Shelby out immensely. A few hours later she was cruising down the streets of Richmond and soon found a parking space a good walking distance from the park. She took a cab the rest of the way since she was back to her game of covering her tracks.

There sat Ian on a park bench in the shadow of Grant's statue. The sight of him made Shelby's heart rate zoom. For now, she stood back watching joggers move down the path, couples smooching on the other benches, and vagrants going through the trash. Each one was a potential agent watching for her—ready to pounce, handcuff, and haul. However, since Ian knew where she lived, setting her up for an arrest made little sense. Unless he was playing two sides of the same coin and was a double agent. If that was true, then he had his own agenda. She had to find out.

It was a frightening scenario. Steadying the camera as inconspicuously as possible, she took several shots of him at different distance settings. Satisfied, Shelby slipped the camera down into the deep pocket and ambled over to him, all the while searching the ground for interesting treats to add to her bag of trash. She picked up crumpled newsprint, a torn mitten, before sorting through a trashcan for a look of authenticity. Adding several more items to her bag, she nearly walked past the bench on purpose. As if an afterthought, she plopped down beside Ian. He ignored her but slid down a few inches in the opposite direction.

"Hey, handsome, gotta buck or two?" She cackled blowing him a kiss.

A cockeyed smile slid up his face in delight. "No, but I'll share my coffee with you. Will Starbucks do?" He passed her his cup. She pushed it back at him. "You're getting better at this; I didn't even recognize you until you sat down. This type of life suits you."

"Great, I've finally found my place in society as a street person."

"That's not what I mean. You're foxy enough to be an undercover agent."

"What a sweet talker. Is this a new FBI tactic called **F**lirting **B**y **I**an?"

He chuckled.

"What's so funny?" She elbowed him.

"Now I know what you'll look like in another forty years."

"Enough flattery."

Ian reached into his coat pocket and pulled out a daisy. Shelby held it up to her nose and closed her eyes for a moment. "I've discovered some very interesting facts about you that need discussing before we can go any further."

"Oh?"

"Tell me your name again."

"Uh-oh."

"Uh-oh is right! There's no agent in the Bureau by the name of Ian Serby. Never was. Tell me, what's that about?" She shuffled about in her brown bag pretending to examine its contents. Selecting something, she tossed a banana peel onto the ground. It was biodegradable.

"Ah, it sounds as if you may have help other than me. Am I right?" He looked at her from the corner of his eye.

"My mother always told me to remain a woman of mystery, especially to strange men. You couldn't be much stranger slipping in and out of my life as you do, coupled with not being the man you claim to be. What I want to know is who you really are and your true name." She offered him a half eaten sandwich with two ants serving as condiments, which he flagged off. Finished with his coffee, he dropped the cup into her bag.

"Fair enough. I'll trade my truth for your trust. My real name is Bernie Epstein. Ever hear of me?"

"No…fill me in."

"I'm sanctioned to be undercover in the FBI. Not everyone in the agency is aware I exist and I lead a small, elite squadron of men. Until recently, I thought they could all be trusted. I was wrong so I went solo."

"Bur-r-r…Bernie, are you an agent who's out in the cold?"

"Hey, you've got attitude. I've always liked that about you. No, I'm not completely out in the cold. Only a certain unit knows about me; some are with me and some are the Wildcards. Within that unit, less than a handful know I'm still alive."

"Doesn't it make it hard on your parents, your family?" Shelby asked.

"My parents are no longer living…and I already told you I have no family. That's what makes my existence so unique."

"Or makes your life nonexistent. It's important to have an anchor in your life." When he didn't respond, Shelby continued, "I hear I'm now at the top of your most wanted."

"Yea, you are. Wasn't my idea, I assure you."

"I can't get over why I am being blamed for

murdering Ms. Waters? Why would I want to do that?"

"Evidentially, as the rumor for the motive goes, she had something valuable that you wanted so you killed her for it. If they arrest you for her murder, then they get what they need and can dispose of you rather easily."

"*What?* Like what?" Suddenly, Shelby remembered the book.

He shrugged his shoulders. "You tell me."

"Look here, the only thing she had that I wanted was her love and her kindness. Can't kill to get that. The most important things in life can't be held in your hand, only in your heart." Shelby fought hard to hold back her tears. "There's nothing worse than a sniveling old woman in the park washing away her disguise. This is frightening for me, Ian…I mean Bernie. Running for my life is one thing but now that I have a bounty on my head, I'm not altogether sure what to do. A million dollars is a lot of money."

"Under-rated. Can't buy a decent country house in the Hamptons. I'd say you're priceless." His voice was soft and meant to comfort her.

"How do I know you're not lying to me again?" Shelby said.

"Listen to me, I know where you live and could have used that information at any time to have you arrested."

"Why haven't you?"

"You're my prize witness. I was going to put you into protective custody but you did a much better job of it than I would have. So I decided to watch over you."

"When will I testify?"

"Just as soon as we start making arrests."

Nerves started drilling away at her insides. "Am I one of the arrests? It seems I'm being framed and my former friend Erin is helping tighten the noose about my neck."

Bernie snapped his head around to look at her in the face, "How did you know about that?"

"Know about what?" Shelby asked, sliding away from him.

"How do you know Erin didn't back you up when Geneen Waters disappeared?"

Shelby wouldn't answer the question. Instead she said, "Perhaps I should run again to avoid being arrested, tried and executed for Ms. Waters' murder. It sounds like the 'bad half' of the FBI is setting me up. Are you sure you're not a part of them?"

"I've all ready told you that I'm not."

"Bernie." She listened to the sound of this new name and shook her head. "Somehow that name doesn't fit you."

"There are people who want to control the outcome of elections."

"Then they need to go to the polls and vote!" When Bernie didn't laugh at her joke, she asked, "Are you referring to the lost software and Top Dog?"

"What do you know?" Bernie narrowed his eyes at her.

"Evidently, I know enough to get me killed." Shelby yearned to lean her head against his shoulder. She felt so stressed that she wanted to sleep for days, just escape.

"You're only a small piece but also one of the most important pieces of a large, growing plot. Think of yourself as the plug in the kitchen sink. You're in over your head with lots of pressure all around. Once we pull you, the whole thing empties out fast."

"You're joking?" She sat up straight and looked at Ian.

"I never joke…but you're safe with me."

"And *you* I can trust?"

"You know you can. I think I've proven that."

"What?"

"I could have taken such advantage of you in the woods and I didn't. Believe me it wasn't easy to stop. Not with you all over me, begging for more."

"I beg your pardon! I was not all over you and I certainly was not begging for more!"

"Ssh, calm down." Bernie looked around and then back at her with that smile of his. "Relax, I was just teasing you. Hey, where's your ring?"

"Oh, my ring." Shelby looked down at her hands. "It must have slipped off…" *and into my drawer.*

"I'll get you another one. I must know where you are at all times. Right now, I would like to know who is helping you."

"What? Don't be so suspicious," Shelby said, stopping to think, "Tell me, who is Top Dog?"

"I can't tell you what I don't know. Ask me something else," Bernie prodded.

"What does the prototype do?"

"It changes election results on the mainframe and is undetectable."

"Are you saying Mondale instead of Reagan could have won?"

"No, it only works in close elections, like Bush and Gore. We don't know whose hands this information is in. Right now, it can go into the hands of the highest bidder."

"But if both parties know about this, then can't the party that doesn't have this microchip cry foul?"

"Only a few men know about it. They aren't interested in which party wins because they couldn't care less. They are interested in the money."

Shelby knew it was foolhardy to stay any longer. She didn't like staying out in the open for long, but it was hard to leave without touching him. Acting on instinct, she leaned in and gave Bernie her best passionate kiss, while slipping a note she had scribbled to him this morning into his pocket. 'I'll hold you in my dreams, until we're together again', it read. Abruptly, she stood up and started to walk away, knowing he was most likely following close behind.

Shelby felt animated, jazzed, and nervous but forced herself to take small stumbling strides in order to keep in character. Should she have a look at Ian's reaction? Perhaps she should just turn around and yell at him right out in the open. If ever she were arrested, she'd claim he made her fall for him. Yep, she'd turn those tables so fast he wouldn't know if it was breakfast, lunch or dinner!

Spinning about, she was shocked. Not only was he not following her, he was no longer on the park bench. In fact, Ian/Bernie wasn't anywhere in sight. He was infuriating.

Shelby jerked open the door of the car. She slid inside and checked herself in the rearview mirror. She did a double take when she saw an old woman staring back at her. Her heart raced until she realized it was only her reflection. Shelby closed her eyes and leaned back, resting on the headrest.

For months, her life had been filled with surprises and betrayal. Each time it made her question the people she had to put her trust in. Her mother had been correct when she said her daughter was about to go on a long journey.

Shelby swiped a tear from her eyes thinking about how she sure would love to pick up the phone right about now and hear her mom's voice. Maybe soon…

Chapter Eighteen

After picking up something to eat, Shelby was back at Sam's and slipped into an old pair of sweats and a T-shirt. She searched the internet for results in city, county, state and national elections for the last thirty years. The statistics were amazing with how many close races and recounts there had been. So a flick of the wrist could tip the number of votes to either side. Bills would be made law by elected officials who weren't really following the will of the people. She squinted, trying to see the screen better. She leaned closer. Bernie was right.

The stats that really interested her were more personal. Rob won the first election by less than three percent of the votes. He won his re-election by a safe margin of twenty percent. Shelby wondered if those figures were honest or the handling of some mainframe juggling the numbers.

Already the light was fading inside the barn and she'd soon be relegated to using the flashlight for the rest of the evening, the computer screen would definitely need to be off. Shelby straddled a stool in front of the flat screen monitor. She rolled her mouse and clicked on the icon for photo software. Working quickly now, she attached the camera to download the pictures from this morning. She couldn't wait to see the images she'd gotten of Ian...no, Bernie...in the park. They came up on her screen nice and clear. A few were too far but there was one good close-up of him.

As the pictures were all coming up, Shelby

realized she was feeling rather chilly. Tonight might be another light freeze and the calendar barely read September. Shelby sprinted back upstairs to put heavy socks on and grab a sweater. After pulling them on, she heard a noise. Footsteps. Someone was moving around downstairs.

It dawned on her she'd left the secret panel open. Trapped she dove into the closet and slipped quietly behind a stack of Sam's moving boxes. Heavy steps thumped up the stairs. More feet pounded the staircase. Ducking as low as she could her chin touched her chest and she wrapped her arms about her. The closet door opened and then something large lunged on top of her. Shelby screamed. A sloppy tongue lapped across her face. "Buddy?"

"Why are you in there?" The deep voice queried.

"What are you doing here, Sam? Isn't there news to report? Or some newsroom emergency to take care of? Next time call me when you're on your way."

"I brought you food but see you've beaten me to it. There are sacks of groceries and melting ice cream on the kitchen counter."

"How was I to know you were bringing food?"

"I left my cell phone for you." Sam held it up for a reminder. "Remember?"

"Yes, I remember!"

"Well, you didn't answer at all and now I know why."

"I needed food." She shrugged her shoulders.

"I said to call me for *anything* and I meant it." Sam didn't try to hide his disgust.

Shelby held up her arms to Sam who pulled her out of the closet. The boxes fell open spilling out clean towels and sheets. They walked downstairs together.

"How was I to know? Talk to me! Tell me your plan! I've been on my own for a long time now and am not used to relying on others," she let him have it.

"You always were an independent soul." Sam stopped abruptly when he saw the picture on the computer screen. "Hey, just where was it you went this morning? And tell me what Adam Bennett's picture is doing on my computer?"

"Adam Bennett? Who's that?" She reeled about, facing the man on the screen.

"Adam Bennett is the former Assistant Director of secret ops for the CIA." Sam pointed at Ian Serby AKA Bernie Epstein. Noticing his digital camera, he picked it up. "Don't tell me you took these?"

"That's Ian Serby." She crossed her arms.

Glancing down at the floor littered with her disguise, he continued. "Shelby, what in the world have you gotten yourself into? I thought you said he was FBI?"

"He told me he was with the FBI, but you say he's with the CIA?" Shelby blinked at Sam. She stood there frozen, unable to feel her feet beneath her. Her cheeks were hot and the back of her neck tightened. In that moment, everything changed.

"*Was* with the CIA. He was in charge of a special ops division overseas but was canned about ten years ago."

"What for?'

"As I understand it, he saw himself as a one man commando unit and didn't want to report his findings to his boss at the CIA, who then accused him of espionage. Nothing was ever proven. If Agent Bennett is meeting you under an assumed name, then it's big. Stop taking chances with your life. Understand?"

"Look here, Sam Oliver, I've been taking care of myself since the day you left me and been doing a darn good job of it, too," Shelby stamped her foot wanting to drop kick Whatzhisname with it right about now. "I just hit a snafu!"

"This is a bit more than a snafu."

"I can't twiddle my thumbs waiting for you to solve this during your free time."

"A little gratitude from you would be nice." Sam steamed as he paced the floor. "I can't figure out why Adam Bennett would be posing as the FBI, unless he is working in tandem with them."

"Maybe he is a covert spy of some kind."

Sam looked at her oddly.

"What kind of a man is Adam Bennett?"Crossly, Shelby tossed out the gooey carton of ice cream.

"Strong and independent. For a time, Bennett was well respected in the CIA, but he never got along with his boss. Some people think accusing Bennett was only a ploy so Epstein could get rid of him."

"*Bernie Epstein*?"

"Yea, the head of the CIA is Bernie Epstein. Very good, now you're catching on. Normally, agents don't divulge anything but you have gotten quite a bit of information from him."

"I sure have. All his pseudonyms." Shelby started picking up her disguise from the floor.

"It sounds as if he's been dropping tidbits of information in your lap. Why does he trust you?" An eyebrow shot up.

"Maybe to give me a sense of false security?"

"Bennett has worked alone for so long that he may see you as a fellow fugitive—wronged by the same people. Maybe he's opening up to you in some perverse sort of way. He may need you more than you need him. I think he's banking on you to restore his reputation."

"I think everyone expects way too much out of me. I would do anything to be able to press a rewind button and call in sick the last week of my Washington internship."

"And if you hadn't overheard the conversation

that day, where do you think you'd be today?"

Shelby sat down on the couch thinking hard on Sam's question. "I still would've walked out on Rob's campaign. I was moving back in with my parents when Bernie and his crew showed up. So perhaps I'd still be there sitting on Mom and Dad's couch watching reruns alongside of them, sending out applications and leading a very uneventful life."

"Listen, I need to get back to Washington tonight. Noah is expecting me." Sam moved toward the door.

"What do you think Sam? Where do you think I would be right now if I hadn't overheard that conversation?" Shelby got up from the couch and took several steps toward him.

Sam paused at the door and then turned to face her. "I'm not sure. But wherever you'd be right now, it wouldn't be on your parents' couch and it sure wouldn't be uneventful."

And like that he was out the door. She ran around the house making sure everything was locked tight and secure. How she wished Sam had stayed the night. Only then would she have been able to completely relax and not wake up with sounds every two seconds.

Shelby ran up the steps to her hiding place and slammed the door.

When will this end? Could Sam and Ian be working together on the same side and if so, which side is that? How do I resolve who he is—Ian or Bernie or Adam?

Shelby felt like a volcano. All her emotions erupted and ran out in tears. Hours later, she woke up with her head on her pillow. She grabbed the clock and looked at the time. She had slept soundly most of the night. It was dawn.

****

Daybreak. The Virginian sun was a yellow disc

in a fall sky. Shelby looked out the back windows toward the Blue Ridge Mountains and sipped her tea while trying to figure out things. Her feelings for Ian were proving problematic. She had to admit she was falling in love with him but now she knew he had been deceptive from the start. Images of them together flashed. She thought of endearing moments with him, flashing them through her mind yet again. Moments like the way he ran his fingers through his hair curling up along his collar line. Then to his advice to stay in the shadows when he lay wounded but still kept his wits enough to hand her his ring so he'd be sure to find her later and keep her safe. There was the time in the foothills of the mountains when they sat below the tree and then how he cared about her missing her parents so he went to enormous lengths to set up the meeting with them. He cared enough to set up a symbol to let her know he was thinking about her, but most of all, she felt safe whenever he was around.

As she chuckled to herself, she couldn't help but ask, "What persona will he take on next?"

Sam was also proving to be a problem. She had allowed him to whisk her away from the cottage too easily. But then again, terror had been a driving force in her life over the past year so she was in the whisking away mode. Now it was time to take back the control and disappear, but first she'd go to her cottage for all her belongings.

No telling what mess she'd walk in to. By now the refrigerated milk would be ready to chew, but she held out hope for her ripening plums. There was also the matter of those spoiled pies setting on the counter. The thought of Jerrica walking in and seeing that mess bothered her. While she packed, she'd also clean.

Sam was on his way to his Washington office and wouldn't be back until late evening. There was time to get it all done. While he had his car, he had left his truck keys right out in plain sight yet again. To do something like that, especially after yesterday, Sam was just asking for trouble.

Shelby parked the truck several blocks from the cottage and walked. She went through the side door into the kitchen. On the table directly in front of her were the half dozen plums in a bowl. At the time, she had bought them they were as hard as stones. She picked one up and gave it a light squeeze. It had nicely ripened and was ready for eating. There on the counter were her pies all shriveled with circles of green mold. The contents of the fridge were unrecognizable. From under the sink, she pulled out a garbage bag and began dumping.

When she walked back into the house from the trash bin, someone waited for her in the kitchen. Startled, her heart rate zoomed. Shelby screamed and narrowed her gaze. It was then she realized it was Ian…Bernie…Adam…oh, Whatzhisname.

There was no one she wanted to see more but she didn't know whether to run out the door or into his arms. Information about him from the last few days flew around in her head, leaving her feeling exposed and raw.

"Sorry I scared you." He leaned against the kitchen counter in the very spot where her pies had been. She could see the muscles in his forearms. What a delicious sight he made.

Not sure what to do, she held her ground. "Next time knock!" Shelby snapped, not taking a step toward him. She liked having half a room between them. It gave her space to think about how to handle this. "You can't just walk in here anytime you please."

He gazed at her intently. "Don't pull out on me now. I've fallen too far in love with you for my own good." He held out his arms to her. With that, Shelby ran to him stumbling over her fear and confusion.

Breathlessly, she looked up into his eyes, her pulse still running hard. “My nerves are frazzled, Ian.”

“What? I thought I told you my name was Bernie?” he asked with an adorable smile.

“Your name *might* be Bernie,” she paused for a dramatic effect, “but you’ll always be Ian to me.”

“Ivy.” Ian said her name as though she belonged to him.

They stood face to face alone in her kitchen. He put both his arms around her and pulled her to him. He said her name again, softly in her ear. It felt good to hear her real name, even if just for a moment. She willed herself to stay strong against his superhuman powers of words and kisses.

“Um, how about I fix us a couple of mugs of green tea?” Shelby spun about, nervously looking through the cabinets.

Ian’s green, symmetrical eyes drifted the length of her body making her feel vulnerable. She yearned to give in to him but she didn’t want to be a pawn in his spy games. She wasn’t up for another heartbreak. “I can’t find the ginger tea.”

“I thought you offered green tea?”

“Oh, that’s right, I did.”

“Forget the tea. I hate the stuff.” And just like that his highly defined arms went around her waist. Her resolve dissolved. She snuggled into him, and as he rocked her in his arms, she smelled soap on his freshly shaven skin. His breath tickled her neck as he kissed her. Yet all she could think about was how he had deceived her time and again so maybe this was all an act, too. Nope, she couldn’t do heartbreak. She stiffened.

Ian sensed a change and pulled back. He held her face in his hands. “What’s wrong? Something has happened.”

"Nothing. I'm tired. I've been hiding for so long that it's finally getting to me." Tears filled her eyes and she cleared her throat. There was nothing more she wanted to do than to call him out on his lies but she was certain he'd counter with brand new ones, all sounding quite believable until she ran them past Sam. Shelby pulled out a kitchen chair from the table and sat down in front of the bowl of plums.

Ian reached into his pocket. He slowly took out a peppermint candy and held it out to her. "Want one?"

Shelby shook her head. Ian shrugged and tossed out the wrapper and put the peppermint into his mouth. In turn she plucked a plum from the bowl and bit into the flesh. The juice filled her mouth. Translucent purple juice slipped from between her lips and dripped onto her blouse. Ian sat silently and fixed his eyes on the spot where the stain hit. She held out a plum to him. Ian shook his head and folded his arms over his chest studying her, while enjoying his candy.

His gaze became disconcerting because she knew him well enough to know he was trying to figure her out. He was wise to do so. She had new information about him and it slightly altered her demeanor putting her in the power seat. Ian was a highly trained agent for some sort of agency somewhere and picked right up on her.

"I found your note in my pocket when I got home."

"And just where is home? Where are you when you aren't hanging around my cottage?"

"The note meant a lot to me."

Suddenly, Shelby felt ashamed over her ungratefulness. "And I love the daisies."

"Do you like them as much as your violas?" Ian suddenly turned mischievous.

"Yes, I do—and they are fast becoming my

flower of choice."

"I just hope you still like these." Ian pointed out the window.

Shelby turned around in her seat trying to see outside.

"Come, let me show you." He took hold of her hand and led her out of the house. In the yard were planted several Viola Sorbet Yesterday, Today and Tomorrow. Ian pulled out the plant stakes and handed them to her.

"They are absolutely beautiful!" She leapt around them imagining Ian walking the aisles of a plant nursery looking for them. It made her laugh.

"I planted them for you this morning."

"I see that."

"Tell me why are these your favorite flowers? Why not something like roses, or orchids?"

"They have always been my favorite because as they grow they change to different hues of blue. But now they take on a new meaning because they remind me of you."

"How so?"

"You change your name much like they change their color." Playfully, she pulled his earlobe.

"By the way, you were gone a long time. Where were you?" Ian's eyes were alive with affection. His sweetness overwhelmed her and Shelby felt her fear falling away.

He snapped his finger at her. "Hey, where did you go just now? I asked where you were all morning."

She reached out her hand to him. "The important thing is that I'm home now—with you."

Quickly, he crossed to Shelby with long even strides and caught her by the shoulders kissing her. His hands tangled in her long hair as they became dancers in their embrace. Ian picked Shelby up and set her on the hard surface, knocking a bowl to the side. Plums rolled every which way, one of them rolled under Shelby's thigh were it was immediately smashed. "Whoa! I think we're making plum jelly!"

Ian laughed so hard that he staggered backward.

Being alone with Ian was too fabulous, too convenient. She had to do something fast, pull the emergency brake on this right now. "By the way, do you happen to have my extra inhaler on you? I've misplaced the one you gave me." Her hand fluttered to her chest and she forced a small cough.

He groaned. "No, I don't. Do you need it? Right now?"

She nodded her head vigorously and purposefully began to hyperventilate.

"I'll be back in about thirty minutes. Wait here?" He pointed.

"Of course." Shelby watched Ian leave by the backdoor. Then down through the yard and over the back fence He disappeared behind the Indian Paint Brush bushes.

She counted five minutes out on the clock above the stove, giving Ian enough time for a good head start. Ian's sudden appearance set her plans back because right now there wasn't enough time to pack a thing. She had to get out of here fast.

Shelby's heart filled with regret as she drove away from her cottage. So many regrets but she had to clear her mind. She had to get her questions answered.

But, how do I deal with my feelings for…oh…Whatzhisname?

Chapter Nineteen

"This may be of personal interest to you." Sam held out the Twin Lakes newspaper. There on the front of the paper was a picture of Congressman Robert Gram with a caption reading MARRIED.

"Married? Married to whom?" In disbelief, Shelby looked at the couple's picture. The bride had short bouffant hair and wore a Vera Wang gown, but those oval shaped eyes were unmistakable. "Erin!" Irritated, Shelby rustled the papers.

"Strange, huh? I guess their love sparked many years ago at the same time ours did." Sam acted nonchalant.

His comments made her stop talking and do a double take. It was refreshing to hear Sam mention their past in endearing terms after hearing nothing but the virtues of his beloved Grace.

Sam caught hold of her hand and flashed a smile. She could have stepped into his embrace and felt his lips on hers for the first time in years. She wondered if they'd feel the same.

"Do you still have that old music box I gave you? You know, the one with the couple dancing?" Sam asked not looking away from her eyes.

Shelby held his gaze. "I think so."

"Do you remember what I wrote on the card?"

"To My Beloved Ivy, All My Love, Sam." Shelby's eyes pooled with tears. In her mind she could hear the music and envision the porcelain couple whirling around and around on the base.

"Ever find out the name of the song it plays?"

Unable to find her voice, she shook her head. Shelby knew their moment to be together had slipped away and remained back in time in a place she could never return to. She had no idea what the future held for her and Ian but she had to find out.

Shelby stepped back. "We're not the same anymore, Sam."

Sam turned red and cleared his throat as he reached for his briefcase.

"I'm sorry, Sam, about just now. You're the best friend I could ever have."

"You're dear to me, too. I have a meeting this afternoon at the station but I can come back tonight if you're lonely," he offered.

"With Noah in the city with his nanny, it's best you stay at your townhouse until the weekend. I'll be fine here and there's always the cell," Shelby held it up.

Sam lingered for a moment at the doorway as if he wanted to say something more. Shelby felt nothing but relief when he left. All ready she had the day planned. Watching Sam drive out in the car, she knew the truck was hers again.

Rain arrived at noon. Only minutes away from the University of Maryland, Shelby chose not to go out in disguise today. Her purpose was to find college records on Erin. Something from her college years and time on their newspaper would answer a lot of questions for her.

Erin's transcripts were a matter of private record but within minutes of strolling into the registrar's office she had a print-off of classes. Shelby focused on the latter years. With a bit of luck, one of the professors might remember Erin from all the other faces. If they could trace her to antigovernment activity, the trip would be well worth the extra miles.

Going over her list of classes and professor's

name, Shelby's puzzlement about Erin's actions increased. As far as political, history, or government classes went, Erin only took the required courses, nothing more, unless one counted the history of the American Theater. For someone truly interested in stepping into politics, it didn't fit. It was just as Shelby had thought; Erin Lowe was theater down to the core with acting classes, directing classes, set design and stagecraft. However, in this one area of championing an underground newspaper, she stepped totally out of character. Shelby read down the list of names and picked her professor of Theater Arts to visit first. She turned right and walked down the hall toward the exit sign, reading the numbers above each doorway trying to locate the right classroom. After she passed a row of windows, she found the correct doorway. Inside was Doctor Morgan finishing up with his morning class. Shelby stood at the back waiting for the room to empty.

"Excuse me," she mused while twirling a lock of fading dyed hair. She smiled sweetly.

"Yes?" the older gentleman answered.

"Hello. I'm trying to find an old friend of mine who worked on a paper here. It wasn't the University paper but another one done by students. Perhaps you remember her and know where I can find her?"

"Her name?"

"Erin Lowe?"

"Erin? Erin Lowe. Did she work on that little grubby paper?"

"Grubby?"

"Yes, it was a loathsome, hideous paper. Thank goodness, it's defunct. No, I have no idea where she is. Sorry, it's been many years."

Drat. Shelby walked out into the hallway and continued down the list of classes on the transcript. Next, she selected the Stagecraft Professor to visit.

When she saw him, he was bent over a large canvas, sketching out a set on the auditorium stage.

"Excuse me, Professor Sugru. I'm wondering if you could help me."

He paused and looked up at her. Giving her his full attention was his answer.

"I'm looking for an old friend from a while back."

"Name, please?"

"Erin Lowe."

"No, the name doesn't sound familiar."

"She wrote for a newspaper while she was here. Not the campus one but another small one."

"Oh, did she work for that cute little paper…oh, what was the name? It was an artsy, government thing…the name? Oh, yes, *The Pledge.* I have no idea where she is now. You might ask Doctor Morgan of Theater Arts."

"Dr. Morgan?"

"Yes, they had a thing going for each other for nearly four years. He sponsored the paper for a bit. The relationship and the paper ended when his tenure was called into question."

And he isn't talking, Shelby mused… "You don't happen to have one of those papers lying around somewhere, do you? I know it's been years."

"As a matter of fact I do," he said with surprise. "I was cleaning out my office closet the other day when I came across a few issues. I was about to throw them out so you came just in time to rescue them. Go take a look if you want; they're back there on a chair near my desk. Just through those doors."

He went back to sketching and she went to snooping. The office was cramped and musty smelling. A window facing east gave her plenty of light to find what she needed. Yes, there they were—five copies on his chair, right on top. *The Pledge.* No time to cruise through them now. Feeling she had the key to unlock the mysteries, Shelby picked up the issues and scooted out of the Fine Arts Building.

Shelby sat in the truck for a moment. Everything in her wanted to tear into the newspapers now but she knew she had been out long enough. Squashing that desire, she turned the key and headed back to Sam's. As she drove, she couldn't help running things through her mind yet again.

"I've gotta figure this out. Years ago at the charity ball something happened to us all. It's like Sam, Rob, Tony, Erin, Karin and I all became a bouquet of flowers tied together with a ribbon. Then one by one, starting with Karin's death, a stem was removed."

"Yet we were all tied together for a purpose. Rob's and Erin's marriage is very suspicious to me. It doesn't fit. I just wish I understood, along with the answer of who murdered Ms. Waters! There are so many loose ends and so much going on here. I've never been able to understand Erin's behavior about her sister's death. She has always been so casual about it. I feel so buttoned up on all sides. I'm more scared than ever. Who can I trust?"

****

After she got back to her room, Shelby read through *The Pledge* papers. It was hard to figure out the underlying meaning of the title, but maybe that was the point. Or maybe there wasn't one. Or was the name a parody?

Page after page of angry prose along with livid looking faces sent shivers down her spine. It was a paper dedicated to unveiling the evils of America. There were marches and protests over international wars, about people starving in the United States, debates about immigration and that was just for starters. The words against the government were filled with hatred supported by flimsy reasoning as well as really bad poetry. Growing up with the bumps and bruises of the working class like she did sure had its advantages; reality was one of those.

Shelby turned back to the computer to research the causes behind the protest marches on the main Wisconsin campus. There certainly had been lots of them; the sixties and seventies by far had the highest numbers. Things seemed to settle down in the decades that followed, until Erin got there to help remind them. Shelby went back and forth between several sites but saw nothing suspicious.

Paging through *The Pledge* Shelby looked closely at the pictures, trying to see a face she recognized. Suddenly, one face did stand out. He had a beard and mustache but it was Ian's. She looked more closely at the picture, trying to make a case that it was someone else, but it was unmistakably Ian. Shelby felt sick. He had been there since the beginning. Ian…Bernie…Adam, whatever name he chose to use didn't matter, the fact remained.

It was time to get out of here. She grabbed her sweater and ran out the door. She jogged down the country road as tears dropped down her face. The chilly wind dried them, leaving her face chapped. Being on the run had made her vulnerable and this Wildcard took full advantage of her. Despite the chilly day, by the time Shelby returned to Sam's, sweat ran down on the inside of her shirt.

From the doorway, she looked across the room at the computer and *The Pledge.* Her research had suddenly turned on her. Shelby pulled bottled water from the refrigerator and returned to her place in front of the computer screen. She opened the paper again to look at the picture. Her first gut reaction was to hold it up under Ian's nose and demand he tell her everything.

Instead she folded it in half and put it into its own folder. She needed it to be kept with the rest of her research in the file box back at the cottage. Shelby steeled her heart for continuing on. With shaking fingers, she typed in *The Pledge*. More than a hundred pages of titles came up for research—books, movies, and more. She continued scanning down, reading more, but the one catching her eye was done at Sam's news station. The title read *Flap Over Presidential Race. Who Really Won?* She read through the article and then printed it out. Research was growing.

After that she decided to double-check election results. A picture of the Washington Monument came up on her screen. She looked at it for a long minute. It reminded her of a monument in Egypt. She had seen a picture of it in the book Ms. Waters gave to her. Shelby printed off everything she had looked at along with personal notes. It was time to take off again.

Chapter Twenty

Shelby returned to the cottage. For too long, she had been separated from the hard drive and Ms. Waters' book. She waited until later in the evening so there were fewer people to be out on the streets and drove the truck within blocks of her cottage, parking it out of reach of the streetlight. From there she walked. The fall air was just crisp enough to make her cheeks tingle as she walked. Seeing her sweet home from afar made her breath catch in her throat. It was so peaceful and welcoming. From habit, she lingered at the gate to pull up a few dead stems.

It was nice to turn the key in the lock of her home and open the front door, even if it was for the last time. Automatically, Shelby turned on extra lights to find everything she needed. The dresser drawers were pulled out one by one and they were emptied into the opened suitcases. She decided to leave some of it behind, to travel as unencumbered as possible. She'd leave tonight in her car but switch license plates. Shelby sat cross-legged on the bed and dumped out all her money from her purse. She lined up the bills and coins, carefully counting it all. It wasn't nearly enough, having spent the bulk of it over the past year. It could last her for a few months. Now that her cash was all but depleted, she'd have to find a job. In the meantime, she'd be frugal.

Standing, she carefully tipped the bedside table so she could get the book on Egypt out. It had served its purpose beautifully in steadying a wobbly leg.

Shelby smoothed out the dent in the cover. For a while she stood staring at it, wondering just how valuable it was. Since she was short on cash, what would it bring on the internet? Ms Waters mentioned it could be worth a king's ransom someday. An idea surfaced...why not offer it up for auction?

She plugged her laptop in and sat in front of the screen. Going to eBay, she typed in the title of the book and pressed enter. To her astonishment, one book like this one was listed. At present the bid was up to hundreds of thousands of dollars. Reading the description, and carefully looking at the pictures, she realized hers was nearly identical. When she got to a safer location, she'd try out her plan.

Shelby pulled the battery plug on her laptop and set it on her bed beside the suitcase. Just like before she began wrapping her clothes around Tony's hard drive and Ms. Waters' book. All that was left to pack was her research. It was then she noticed she had turned on nearly all the lights. Darn it. Shelby hurried between rooms and turned off the extra lights.

Suddenly, there was pounding at the front door. It could be Ian; she did tell him to knock next time. She gulped feeling sick inside her stomach. Quickly, she set the suitcases and laptop case along with her purse behind the bathroom door and tried opening the window. It was jammed. Tiptoeing down the hallway, she opened the curtains an inch and peered out. It was Jerrica and she was using her realtor key to open the lock. Shelby unbolted the door and flung it open. Jerrica stepped back with surprise.

"Shelby! Sam said you were gone." Clearly, she was stunned. "I saw all the lights on so I thought I'd knock first but when no one answered..."

"I am almost gone. I just came back for my personal things." Shelby looked in the direction of the bathroom.

"Then I can rent the cottage?" Jerrica took a professional tone.

"Of course." It was then she noticed the young woman standing beside Jerrica under the porch light.

"This is Betty Lou," Jerrica explained. "She lost the lease on her rental property at Dusty Trails Trailer Court and asked if I had an available property. I'm here to show her around," Jerrica explained.

"Betty Lou, I believe we met several months ago. I bought something from you at a garage sale…and aren't you the one who occasionally watches Noah Oliver?"

"Yes, I do watch Noah. Sam is a great guy."

"That he is. Please, come on in." Shelby stepped aside.

Betty Lou immediately started opening and closing closets doors and cabinets. Jerrica followed along as she explained the history of the house. She also pointed out the crown moldings and mentioned the square footage of the cottage. Betty Lou stopped listening and switched her attention to Shelby who was shoving papers into a file box.

Shelby accidentally dropped a folder. The papers drifted across the wooden floors. "I'll get them!" She quickly flagged the two women away not wanting either to get a peek. Casually, Betty Lou bent over and picked a paper and handed it back to Shelby. It was the wanted poster with the one-million-dollar reward for her capture. Shelby quickly looked up at Betty Lou but she had disappeared into the kitchen.

Just as Shelby finished with the last of the papers, Betty Lou stuck her head around the corner of the room and with a mischievous smile said, "Hey, *Ivy*, I do love how you decorated this place."

Shelby replied with a broad smile, "I can't take

credit; it was really done like this before I moved in here."

Jerrica looked oddly at her former tenant. "Ivy? Who is Ivy?"

Shelby blanched. "Ah, what did she call me? Silly me, I wasn't paying any attention. I'll just answer to any name."

For now, Jerrica seemed to swallow the thin reasoning as Betty Lou went to have her second look at the summer porch. Shelby started to follow her out, when Jerrica stepped in front of her. "I thought we were friends."

"We are friends." Shelby sounded unconvincing. She was more preoccupied with what Betty Lou might be up to and tried to skirt around Jerrica, who held Shelby in place by grabbing her arm..

"Apparently, our friendship means little to you. You breeze into town and then out again without a word of goodbye. Would you please pay attention to me while I talk?"

Shelby nervously licked her lips. "There are things I can't explain right now."

"Why not?" Jerrica tapped her foot.

Betty Lou walked back into the room. Jerrica smiled. "Betty Lou, let me show you the bedrooms. They're quite spacious for an older home, that is."

"No thanks. I think I may be buying something soon instead," Betty Lou explained. "I just found out I'm about to come into a chunk of change."

An alarm went off inside Shelby as hairs rose at the back of her neck and along her arms. The time to leave was right now. She had to get her gear from the bathroom into her car that was still parked at the side of the house and peel out of town as fast as she could. "Excuse me. There's something I need to tend to at the back of the house," Shelby calmly went down the hall as the sound of sirens started to whine through the night.

Walking out the front of the house without being seen was an improbability. Shelby began breathing hard. Where was her inhaler? Shelby opened her purse but didn't see it. There was no time left. Shelby tried the bathroom window one last time. It still wasn't budging. Shelby hooked her purse strap over her neck, tucked her laptop under her arm, picked up her suitcases and went back down the hall, past the two women, and out the back door. Just as she reached her car, a police officer sitting in a cruiser turned the spotlight on her. He radioed for back-up as he got out.

Handcuffed, Shelby was walked back into the house that was already filled with officers. Like Betty Lou had, they were going through cabinets and closets. Fortunately, they hadn't spotted her file box yet tucked behind the computer stand.

Chatty Betty Lou was standing in the middle of the room. "See? This is her picture. I think it looks like her, don't you?" Betty Lou held up the wanted poster. "Ah and there she is now!"

Everyone turned to look at her. Her time as Shelby was over. Feeling dizzy, the floor seemed to drop away.

****

When she came to, Ivy found herself lying on her bed. There were only a couple of police officers in the room and they weren't paying attention to her. She hoped to somehow slip out and with all the commotion in the house, she figured it was worth a chance. Ivy tried sitting up but was immediately jerked back by a metal object locked on her left wrist. The two officers turned to look at her but didn't say anything.

Ivy's heart pounded weakly as she looked toward the hall and saw the disillusioned expression on Jerrica's face. Her friend spoke in a monotone, "I didn't know she was a fugitive. How would I know about that? As far as I'm concerned, she was just another tenant passing through town." She looked at Ivy and shook her head. Jerrica's eyes filled with tears. Ivy couldn't tell if they were tears of compassion or fury.

Betty Lou walked into the room. "Who is in charge here anyway? I need to speak to someone about my reward. I really need it *now*," she demanded.

When no one responded, Betty Lou walked out and her voice could be heard in the other room, "Whoever is in charge, would you please step up? We have a matter to settle here."

"Where will I be taken tonight?" Ivy asked one of the officers.

"We're waiting on the FBI to get here. A special agent in charge of your case will be here soon."

"Did someone mention my name?" Ian breezed into the room and flashed his credentials along with a smile. "Ivy Dillon, I'm Adam Bennett. Men, we have been all over the East trying to catch this gal. Good work, but I'll take over from here. Key for the handcuffs, please?"

He unlocked the cuff from the bed and then cuffed both arms behind her back. "How are you doing, my dear?" he whispered in her ear.

"I need my stuff," she whispered back.

"Where?"

"Ask the police. I have two suitcases, my purse and laptop." Deliberately, she didn't mention the file box. All her research was in there about the murder along with her written notations and the picture of Adam as one of the Wildcards. That had to get into Sam's hands.

"Officer, keep an eye on her and make sure she doesn't escape, all right? She looks sweet but she's filled with fire." A smile slid up the side of his face and he gave her a slow wink. Moments later, Adam was back with the items. He held them up as if to ask if he had gotten the right items. She nodded. "Has anyone opened or removed anything from these items? If so, I need to know immediately."

"No, sir, it's all there. Nothing has been opened or looked at."

"Now who is the person who made the phone call?" Adam looked around.

"I am! Are you the one in charge?" Betty Lou pushed forward. Her face was flushed with excitement and she held out her hand. Not for it to be shaken but expecting cash to be placed in it.

"There is a matter of a reward for you. Be sure to give your name and all your information to any one of the officers here tonight. I'll get in touch with him in the morning. We'll cut you a check as soon as this person has been verified as actually being the Ivy Elizabeth Dillon we are looking for."

"Yippee!" She jumped up and down and then stumbled backward on her heels falling over a chair.

"Wait, I need to say goodbye to Jerrica," Ivy begged Adam.

Adam spoke softly, "There's no time. We have to get out of here before the FBI arrives."

"Jerrica!" Ivy hollered toward the hall. "You told me to remind you about your file box."

Jerrica walked into the room. She looked confused. "File box?"

"Yes, your file box with all your information on house listings? In all this excitement, you may forget it here and then Sam will be upset with you if you do not show the new horse property listing inside of it. So much time has been spent putting together that information for Sam and it should be given to him and only him."

Jerrica slowly nodded with understanding and said, "Did you see where I left it?"

"Yes, it's in the living room behind the

computer."

"That's right." Jerrica headed in that direction.

"Would someone walk Ms. Dillon to my car out front?" Adam queried. "I'm carrying her belongings, which are now federal evidence."

Adam led the way while an officer followed with Ivy. For a moment she hung back, not wanting to step into the dark sedan that waited for her at the curb like a hearse. As if reading her mind, he whispered into her ear, "It's all right. Trust me one more time."

When he opened the rear door to his sedan, she slipped inside. The blackness swallowed her. There was no moon tonight so when Ivy looked out the car window at the porch light it was as if it was her last salvation. Seeing that solitary light actually gave her comfort.

Adam got into the driver's seat and slammed the door. "Your belongings are safe in the trunk." Then he accelerated down the street. Within minutes they were on the interstate.

Chapter Twenty-One

He glanced at her in the rearview mirror.

"Where have you been, Ivy?"

"What do you mean?"

"Where have you been since the cottage? You sent me out for the inhaler and then left. Why? I didn't know if the Wildcards had picked you up or if you were on the run again." He turned his head for a moment to look at her. "I was scared out of my mind."

"Here we go with the Wildcard talk again." Ivy rolled her eyes. "Are you one of them?"

"Your question wounds me," he whined comically.

"Tell me about the Wildcards."

"You know it as well as I do. The mission of the Wildcards is to find the missing microchip that was engineered by a group of scientists. It's my job to ferret them out and find that chip."

"Mainframe, too," Ivy said.

"What?"

"Don't forget about the missing mainframe!" Ivy raised her voice at him.

"Oh, I do love how you sass. It's what won my heart," Adam grinned. "You're usually right but not in this case. Only the microchip is missing."

"Don't forget about the prototype. That is missing, too." Ivy looked around. "Tell me how they work together."

"All three are essential. Placed in different locations they are nearly undetectable. The microchip is to be implanted in the machines at voting polls; the election results are manipulated through the mainframe at a central location. This will decisively throw the race one way or another in close elections."

"How close?" Ivy asked.

"Less than ten percent. For landslides, it'll never work. In that scenario, it would be easily detected that something had been rigged due to pollsters before the election and exit polls."

"Exit polls are flawed. Don't you watch the news?"

"Ha, I remember when I asked you that same question the day we informed you about Ms. Waters' death."

"If you can control who is in office, then the laws of the nation are also controlled. With so many close races, I say our nation is pretty evenly divided. I, for one, am pretty tired of all those hanging chads."

"We were close to picking up someone when there was a break-in at the Chicago headquarters and the evidence we needed was taken," Adam explained.

"The Chicago FBI headquarters was broken into?"

"No, Congressman Robert Gram's re-election headquarters."

Chills ran over her arms and down her spine. Ivy wondered if he was referring to her break-in of Tony's computer when she snatched his hard drive. "What does Rob have to do with this?"

"Nearly everything." Adam sounded certain.

"You should have told me that a long time ago."

"And you should have stayed put when I told you to!" Adam took a breath and then spoke softer, with measured words, "Good buddy Tony Bogart along with Congressman Robert Gram conspired together about taking America from the inside out by means of the voting booth. With this information, they planned to become very wealthy men. The FBI, CIA and Homeland Security look for bigger deals going down from the outside coming in to our country. John Doe and his vote at the polls have been overlooked."

"Where are we going?"

"What I want to know is where you've been? Do you know how crazy with worry I was about you?"

"I hate it when you do that."

"Do what?"

"Ignore my questions because you're too preoccupied with your own agenda. Where are we going?"

"I am taking you to my home. You'll be safe there."

"And where is your home?" Ivy moved around trying to find a comfortable spot to rest her back. The handcuffs were starting to cut-off circulation and her back ached.

"New York. Now will you answer my question?"

"I needed distance between us. You confuse me with all the aliases you use. I have no idea who you really are."

"It doesn't matter what name I use."

"Now you're Adam Bennett...but who is Adam Bennett?"

"My resume is long and complicated. All that matters is what I am doing now. Someone has put me on this case, someone high in office. Ivy, everything I've told you is the truth."

"Everything?" Ivy asked.

"I love you, Ivy. And I vow to keep you safe. Believe that most of all. You, however, have not been forthcoming with what you know."

"Yes, I have!" Ivy insisted.

"No, you're protecting someone." Adam looked into the rearview mirror. "I hope it's not Sam

Oliver."

"Sam is none of your business!" Ivy straightened her back.

"Oh, but he is my business. Your former fiancé."

"How do you know about that?" Ivy asked with surprise.

"When it comes to you, I know everything."

"Well, I know a few things about you, too. I saw a copy of *The Pledge*."

"*The Pledge?* Wow, you are good at this spy stuff." Adam seemed delighted.

"Your picture is in it."

"That doesn't surprise me. I was working undercover at that time."

"Is that why you have so many nom de plumes?" Ivy moved around uncomfortably. "Just how long will you be keeping me handcuffed? My back is killing me."

Adam took the next exit and drove for a few miles until he found a less traveled road before pulling off to the side. As soon as he got out of the car, he opened the rear door and helped Ivy out. He turned her around and placed the key into the lock, twisting and unlocking the handcuffs before tossing them into the backseat. He spoke quietly in the darkness as he slammed the door, "Sorry about the cuffs. Ride up front with me." He opened the passenger door for her.

They pulled back onto the interstate and drove for over thirty minutes in silence. She watched Adam's profile in the dashboard light trying to figure him out, praying he was really a good guy and wondering why she was falling in love with someone she really didn't know. She kicked something on the floor by her feet. Ivy pulled up a gadget. "What's this?" She held it up.

"That, my dear, is a voice machine. You snap it onto a phone and when you talk it modifies the sound of your voice," Adam told her.

"The 'Voice' might have used a machine like this. I told you about him when I was in your apartment the day my apartment was burgled." She looked at Adam. His smile was thin. Given the look on his face and what he wasn't saying, Ivy had to ask, "Adam, are you the 'Voice'?"

"I am."

Fear ran through her veins. She had to escape. Ivy reached for the door handle considering leaping from the car the moment it slowed. She watched the ground go by at more than sixty miles an hour. "Where are you really taking me?"

"I already told you." His attention remained on the road.

"You called over and over again. Why? No matter how many times we moved or changed our phone number you found Erin and I." Ivy fought back tears. She was angry at Adam for tricking her, mad at herself for loving him. Her chest burned. That meant she had given herself over to panic. Her throat was swelling. Ivy began counting slowly, trying to slow her breathing. She trained her eyes on the speedometer.

"My cover at the paper was eventually blown so I needed to find someone within the framework of the organization to be my snitch. From my days of working on *The Pledge,* I knew Erin was the weakest link but I also knew she would have no part of it. Finally, after a couple of years, she vanished. It took me by total surprise. I suspected she had changed her name. I didn't find her again until I happened to see a picture of her in the cast of a new play. Bingo, I had Erin." He shook his head. "I followed the cast to the party that night where you handed me your new phone number with the address on your card. That quixotic slip-up put me right back in business. Within hours, I was living in an apartment right above you, but when you found me, I moved right back out." Adam pulled over to the side of the road and stopped the car. "Get out."

"What?" Ivy looked around at the headlights from the traffic flowing by. Beyond were fields of nothingness covered in night.

"Your hand is on the door handle and you've been watching my speed. Obviously, you feel your life is in jeopardy. I don't want you to jump out while the car is moving. It's unsafe. Get out." Adam steamed.

Ivy took her hand off the door handle and stared straight ahead.

"Okay, you had your chance." Adam bolted from the car and went around the back. Ivy watched the side mirror but he wasn't in view. In a moment, she felt trunk slam closed. When Adam got back into the car, he tossed her the inhaler from her belongings and then pulled back onto the interstate.

"Thanks." Ivy used the inhaler. Adam was a good talker. Her flaw was she always believed what he said. She prayed it wouldn't be her fatal flaw.

"You're tired. Lay your head back in the seat and relax. I'll wake you when we're close."

"Adam, I'm sorry. I didn't understand and it's just..."

"Stop. It's all right." His answer was short and he wasn't in good humor.

****

It seemed as if she had just closed her eyes when Adam shook her awake. Ivy rubbed her eyes and looked at the car clock. It was only two a.m. Adam had already taken her belongings so she followed him into the house. The furnishings were standard Goodwill. She frowned when she realized there was just one bedroom with a twin bed. Totally exhausted Ivy yearned for a large bed to stretch out in, but right now, any bed would suffice. Adam placed several blankets with a pillow on top of the laundry basket in the bathroom. Ivy could only imagine how uncomfortable it would be for him to sleep in the tub.

"Go ahead and use the facilities." He stepped aside.

Ivy welcomed the warm bath. Afterward when she was brushing her teeth, it suddenly occurred to her that Sam would be frantic about her safety. She had to call him now. Surely, Adam would understand this. Pulling on the doorknob, it wouldn't budge. She twisted the lock and still it wouldn't open.

"Adam!" she tapped at first. "The door is stuck."

"It's not stuck. It's locked," he said from the other side. "I'll see you in the morning."

"Let me out!" She formed her hand into a tight fist and hit the door.

"I'm dog tired and can't take a chance of you slipping out on me while I sleep."

"Adam! I would never do that." Anxiety came flooding back.

"Oh yeah? Well, it took me days to find you this last time and you were nearly picked up by the Wildcards. Nope, I'm not letting you out of my sight again."

Panicked, Ivy looked through her things; thankfully, nothing was taken.

"All your belongings are still intact. See you in the morning...try to make yourself comfortable. Goodnight, my love."

Ivy was so furious she refused to answer. Here she was trapped in another windowless room. What would he do to her in the morning? More importantly, what would *she* do to him in the morning for locking her in here?

Am I falling in love with a maniac? Or am I the crazy one?

Chapter Twenty-Two

There was a terrible crick in her neck. The stay overnight in the darling claw-foot tub had not done her any favors. Her back ached terribly. A stream of sunlight fell through the open doorway. Wrapping the blanket about her, she walked barefoot out into the bedroom. The bed was already neatly made. Ivy snooped a bit and found his clothes were neatly hung in the closet and all the dresser drawers had items neatly folded inside of them. Ivy never figured Adam as a tidy sort of guy.

The aroma of brewing coffee pulled her in the direction of the kitchen where Adam waited. “Grab yourself a mug from the cabinet. I just brewed us a pot.”

“No thanks.” She sat down. Her lips pursed in a thin line. “I like to smell coffee, not drink it.”

Adam pulled open the small refrigerator door. “Orange juice?”

Ivy nodded. He poured her a tall glass and set it down on the table in front of her. “Are you still mad over spending the night in the latrine?” Adam touched her hand but she pulled away. “I guess I know the answer to that question.”

“I’m hungry.” Ivy stared straight into his eyes.

“There are warm eggs in the pan on the stove. Help yourself.”

Ivy went to the counter and noticed a clean plate with a fork laid out for her.

“Finish them up. I’ve already had my breakfast and I hate waste.”

Ivy saw his empty plate in the sink. After scooping the last of the eggs onto her plate, she seated herself in the same spot, across from Adam. She couldn't ever remember being so hungry.

"Tell me something about you that I don't already know."

Adam suddenly seemed to have turned soft and dreamy eyed. No way could she look at him for long without feeling that way herself so she salted her eggs. "Actually that's a question I'd like to ask you." Ivy looked up through the tops of her eyes at Adam, knowing he wasn't about to talk about himself. She loved turning his own words back on him and hoped if she opened up he would open up, too.

After a quick sigh, she began, "My dad built me a sailboat. It took him a full winter using up all of his free time to complete it in time for summer. The first time I took it out on the lake, I ran it aground and put a big hole in the stern. I was so afraid he was going to be mad, but he wasn't. Instead we pulled it up to our yard and we worked on the repairs together. We didn't say much but it was just being together that really mattered."

"I like that image of you and your dad together, especially since I've met him."

"Okay, your turn. Tell me something I don't know about you."

"I don't know what to say." Adam shook his head.

"You have a whole life; pick one thing to tell me."

"I'd rather talk about us." He reached across the table.

"And I'd rather talk about the investigation."

"Talk away." Adam crossed one arm over the other.

"Last night you said something about Sam being part of the voting plot."

"In all honesty, I don't know where Sam fits in to this scheme." Adam sat back as though he suddenly wanted to surrender. He looked tired, more tired than she even felt. "This I do know, my investigation keeps taking me back to Congressman Gram. It's like a roundabout trying to pin him down. Take the wrong turn and you're shot off in the wrong direction of where you need to be."

"Did you know Tony Bogart took money from the campaign?"

"How much did he take?" He raised his shoulders.

"A lot. Eighty to one hundred thousand dollars, maybe a bit more."

"Ha, you just disproved one of my theories. In some circles, that's a lot of money but it doesn't even cover the cost of a good wedding, certainly not our wedding."

"Wedding? There is no 'our wedding'," Ivy huffed. Mad at Adam for all his lies and deceptions, she decided to sting him. "Whatever might have been between us is done. I used you as much as you used me."

"Fair enough." Adam stared at her coldly.

"What do you need in order to wrap this case up?" Ivy asked.

Adam cleared his throat and settled back in his chair. "First and foremost, I need to know the leader's identity and where the software is right now. Also how is this plan going to be implemented? How will the software be installed—in the factory or on site? If they install on site, that means a lot of manpower spread out. Then trust becomes an issue. How are the machines maintained and monitored? Then do they plan on having someone at every polling place?"

"That seems unlikely to me. Too much can go wrong."

"That's my thinking, too. I'm sure the coded signal will be sent to the mainframe but I won't know for sure until I see the plans."

Praying she wasn't making the biggest mistake of her life, she asked, "Would Tony Bogart's hard drive answer some of your questions?"

"If I could get my hands on Tony Bogart's hard drive, I sure wouldn't refuse a look."

Ivy got to her feet and hurried down the hall. Within five minutes she was back, wearing a fresh set of clothes. "I'm a fast dresser." She curtsied, by now sorry she had hurt him.

"I see." He tried not to smile at her.

"It's your birthday today, isn't it?" Ivy flirted, trying to get back in his good graces.

"Why? Do you have a present for me?" His eyes sparkled.

"Yup, I do. Here is Bogart's hard drive." She handed it to him. "I didn't have time to wrap it."

"*You* had it all this time? *You?*" Adam reached out for it and Ivy quickly put it behind her back.

"But it's my birthday!" he sweetly protested.

"It's also mine." She swayed, stepping next to him.

"What do you want?"

"I want to call Sam and let him know where I am."

"Oh Sam. The great love of your life!" Adam angrily spit out as he rose from his chair.

Ivy decided not to correct him. "By the way, where in New York are we?"

"Delaware." Adam snatched the hard drive and went to his computer.

"Delaware! You said we were in New York." Ivy followed behind him dogging his steps.

"Well, we're not. Go ahead and use my phone to call Sam. Happy birthday to you, too!" he yelled.

"I don't get you, Adam."

"That's quite obvious." Adam turned and stood toe to toe with her. "It's what you want, isn't it? To call Sam? So...go call him."

She spotted her personal file box on the floor next to the computer. It had been opened and her research had been divided into piles. "How did you get that?" Ivy narrowed her gaze at him.

"I took it out of Jerrica's hand. I knew by the way you were acting that it was part of the case. By the way, good work." Adam removed the hard drive from his desktop and inserted Bogart's in its place. On the screen was a symbol of a microphone with bolts of lightning shooting through it. Ivy moved closer for a better look.

"What an awesome icon. It must be their mantra. Let's see what it does. Wow, there's a Trojan Horse on this for sure." Adam whistled.

"A what?"

"A back door. This hooks up to thousands of emails all over the United States. I'm salivating here. There's social security numbers, names, occupations. Bingo! Part of the whole darn shooting match is right here! You've had it all along!" Adam leapt up from the computer and threw his arms about Ivy. "I love you, Ivy! We're going to have such a great life together as soon as you realize Sam is totally wrong for you. I'm the one you really want." Then he sat back down and returned to work.

"Then it was worth protecting the disk even after what Tony did to me."

Adam spun about in his chair and turned deadly serious. "After he what? What did Tony do to you?"

"Tony knocked me around a bit." Ivy shivered remembering the terrible night.

Adam stood to his feet and gently held her by the shoulders. "Are you sure you're all right?"

"I am now."

"I'll get him for you by making sure he's locked

behind bars forever. He and his cohorts are committing treasonous acts but I'll make sure he's also charged with assault." Adam returned to the computer. He kept taping out numbers and names, one window opened up another and then another.

"That all looks so complicated." Ivy couldn't take her eyes from the screen.

"Let me explain it to you. Here look…you can type the search pattern in the edit box. While you are typing, Wildcard Select tells Explorer to select all the files from the current window that match the pattern. If you press Cancel or erase the pattern, Wildcard Select restores the original selection. If one or more files were selected at the time you invoked Wildcard Select, it will only try to match the items from that selection. I think this is how the votes are changed."

"What now?"

"Now, I am going into choice computers all over the country to see what has been sent and what is written." His eyes zigzagged all over the screen searching, reading, as his fingers tapped out his commands. "Why, lookie here, I have correspondence."

"Can you read emails that are inside other computers?"

"Absolutely. All I need is their email address and password and that's right here, too." He laughed as a madman, releasing joy over finally gleaning years worth of work. "With this I can break into any of these computers and send email which will look as if it came from their mailbox." Adam blew on his fingertips as if he were a safe cracker.

"Will anyone be able to tell you were in there?"

"Nope, it's another beautiful aspect of this. I'm invisible. So this is how they communicate without ever having to meet face-to-face. There are computer patches that people innocently install on their machines thinking it safe guards them from hackers, when what it really does is open up a window so hackers can see precisely what is going on. Ever take an online survey?"

Ivy nodded.

"The online voter surveys we take are piped into one area for analysis so those running for office will have a better idea of what to say and it helps target the party liners from residence to residence. It's more accurate than an Exit Poll. Do you know how you threw them off course by taking this item? It's taken a long time for them to regroup. It's a sheer miracle you're still alive!" Adam jumped up from the computer and twirled Ivy around the room.

Ivy laughed and threw her arms around Adam's neck. Just as he found her mouth to kiss her, she asked, "Is Sam's name in there?"

"No, I didn't see it."

"Sam is as honest as they come," Ivy confirmed.

"Go, call your Sam!" His face crumpled, as he waved her off. Adam returned to the computer. His fingers snapped hard against the keys.

"You can't stay mad at me, Adam, I know you."

"What makes you say that?" he asked with his back toward her.

"Because you love me."

Adam's fingers stopped moving. "Loving you hasn't been easy."

Ivy kissed his forehead and went to the phone. A few hours later Sam thundered up the steps and into Adam's house like a storm.

Chapter Twenty-Three

Finally, Sam and Adam met face-to-face. Ivy braced herself for a battle, but all the distrust for one another seemed to be in the past now as they sat in Adam's house talking to one another. Adam explained that seven years ago he was commissioned by the President of the United States to complete the investigation into voter fraud. It made total sense to Sam.

Sam reacted as though he and Adam were lifelong buddies. Admiration for one another's work bloomed and Adam showed Sam the disk. They sat together, backs turned to Ivy, in front of the computer. To Adam's explanations, Sam kept nodding and slapping him on the back as if he were an old high school football chum.

"Let's make several hard copies for safekeeping," Sam suggested. "Meanwhile, let's get that puppy printed out for me to read."

"We'll have to buy a printer. Mine is shot."

"I'm sure I can get it going again," Sam offered standing up to look at it. "I'm pretty good at fixing these things."

"No, mine is literally shot. I was cleaning my gun and it went off...hitting my machine. See? I need a new one."

They rode in Sam's BMW; Adam sat in the front beside the driver and Ivy sat in the back with her feet up on the soft leather seat. The late fall air was at the freezing mark, the sky threatened snow. Sam cranked up the car's heater.

"You know, Ivy, if you had just waited to go to the cottage until I came with you, the police and FBI wouldn't be looking for any of us right now," Sam sputtered.

"I agree with you, Sam," Adam nodded. "Ivy wanted to take off again and needed the rest of her stuff. Fortunately, I picked up the police call or she'd be in FBI custody right now along with the hard drive."

"Thank God Adam found you."

"Yes, thank God for Adam. And thank God for you, Sam. Now will you two stop picking on me?" Something caught Ivy's eye out the window. Something she didn't want to see. "Hey, go around the block again, okay?" She tapped Sam's shoulder.

"Why?" Adam asked.

"I think I just saw Mitchell."

"Who's that?" Sam asked turning the car around.

"Someone from my team who's playing for the other side," Adam snapped.

"He's the one who set up the ambush that nearly killed Adam. I was the next name on his list," Ivy said. "Mitchell was standing at that gas station back there and he was looking at a map. It sure looked like him but it's hard to tell since he wasn't in his signature dark suit."

Sam drove them past the station but this time Mitchell was nowhere in sight.

"Let's cruise back down my street, but not too slowly."

There was a car parked in front of Adam's house and the front door to his house was open.

"That was the car I saw Mitchell standing next to back there. Good thing I have the hard drive right here on me, huh guys?" Ivy grinned.

"Sam, we need to leave the area. Be sure to do the speed limit," Adam warned.

“Where to now?” Sam wanted to know, turning back on the highway.

“Maybe we can go back to your house, Sam,” Ivy suggested.

“There’s no way I can go back home. I’m sure they’re searching for all of us everywhere, but especially around Washington D.C.,” Sam said.

“You should be all right, Sam. It’s Adam and me who are in trouble.”

“Not anymore. Evidently, all my questions at the FBI raised suspicion. When a background check was run on me, they came up with my engagement to you, Ivy. Both my houses have been searched and they found your belongings in the barn,” Sam explained.

“Sam, what about Noah and his nanny?” Ivy felt alarmed.

“Jerrica took them into an empty house of hers for now. My parents are arranging for them to go across the Canadian border and stay with friends until this is over.”

“We need to lay low for a while and get to a safe house for tonight,” Adam said.

“I’m starving. Can we lay low while eating?” Ivy patted her stomach.

Sam drove thirty minutes south before stopping for lunch. Without a coat or sweater, Ivy felt frozen by the time they parked the car and hurried inside the restaurant. She ran her hands over the tops of her arms trying to warm up. She hadn’t planned on this turn in the weather, but it came nonetheless.

After eating, they decided to drive into Maryland and then try to make it in to see the President at the White House by midnight with the evidence. Opening the door to go back outside, the parking lot was fast filling up with sleet and snow.

“Wait right here and I’ll get the car.” Sam loped off through the lot, slipping once along the way.

Just as he pulled up to let Adam and Ivy into the car, they saw Mitchell in his car motoring down the street. Panic set in. Adam pulled open the rear door for Ivy before Sam had completely stopped the car. She slipped on the ice dropping her purse, which went under the right rear wheel of the car. They all heard the crunch at once. Sam slammed the gearshift into park and jumped from the car thinking he had run over Ivy who lay inches from the tire.

Adam and Sam helped her to her feet and into the car. Ivy was inconsolable as she reached inside her purse and pulled out the crushed disk. "For so long I've protected this and just when it matters the most I break it."

"Technically, it was me who broke it." Sam was sullen. He drove down the street and back onto the interstate with no destination in mind.

"What now?" Ivy lamented.

"I guess I continue with my investigation," Adam said. "What about you, Sam?"

"I'm going into hiding with my family for now. You're coming too, Ivy."

"No thanks, I'm on my own."

Adam turned around to face Ivy, "I still need your testimony."

"Forget you!"

Adam's voice was soft and low. "Don't ever think with your emotions. Use your head, always. It's the only way you will survive."

"Ivy, your money is about gone. There's no way you can survive this time without help," Sam added.

"Pardon me, but there's one more ace up my sleeve." She pulled the book of maps from her purse and waved it up in the air. "I just saw a book like this one on eBay going for hundreds of thousands of dollars. I'll be just fine. See? I am using my head."

Adam reached for the book. "Let me see that."

Ivy passed it over the seat to him and explained, "Ms. Waters gave it to me as a parting gift. At first, I thought it might contain the prototype or a chip but I carefully examined each page. Nothing is in there."

A creased piece of paper fell from between the pages. Adam unfolded the paper and studied the writing. "This is hieroglyphics. Let's go to the Smithsonian and see if a curator can decipher it."

The roads became an icy mix. Further south the mix turned into melting slush. They arrived at the museum thirty minutes before closing. Adam flashed his FBI badge and the place was theirs. The museum's expert Egyptologist was at their disposal.

"Can you decipher this for me?" Ivy slid the paper across the table to the gentleman.

He read it silently with great interest displayed on this face before removing his glasses. "Fairly basic, really. It reads, 'Lady Ivy, the obelisk is closer than you think. I enjoyed our talk.'"

With a deep sigh, Ivy pulled back from the table. "Well, it does answer one question; Ms. Waters is the author of the note. She's trying to tell me something but I can't figure it."

"I haven't a clue." The curator blinked.

"What's an obelisk?" Sam asked.

"It's a monument that the first lady pharaoh of Egypt had built," the curator explained.

"Hatshupset was her name," Ivy clarified.

"Yes. She was known for building. Actually, at the time, she had two built and intended to have them both covered in gold to reflect the setting sun, but it was grossly expensive, so only the tips were covered in gold. There once were two obelisks, however, now, the one remains. It's still the tallest monument in Egypt at fifty feet high."

"There's a picture of it in here. I'll show you." Ivy paged through the book and stopped when she saw the tall four-sided building that came to a pinnacle at the top.

"You know what this looks like to me?" Sam asked.

"Yes, I certainly do," Ivy replied. "The Washington Monument."

Back in the car, Adam reasoned, "Now we know why the other book is going so high on eBay. Ivy, the Wildcards think it's the book Ms. Waters had, and they think like you once did, that the microchip is hidden in it. That's why you are being blamed for killing Ms. Waters! If they have you, they have the book." Adam carefully went from page to page and bent each one.

"Hey, what are you doing!" Ivy screamed at him. "The papers are very delicate and you are breaking them. Look, they are crumpling!"

"I just want to be sure the microchip hasn't been implanted inside the pages," he said ignoring her concern.

"All you need to do is hold the pages up to the light, or run your fingers over the pages!" Ivy yelled. "And I all ready did that!"

"This is better," Sam said. Then he pulled out his pocketknife and opened up the spine. Nothing.

"Well, you certainly ruined my gift and my hope of selling it on eBay." Ivy angrily looked at the tattered book in Sam's hands. "What will I do for money now?"

"One more stop. Let's go to an antique shop," Sam suggested. "I want to look at the note from Ms. Waters under a black light. Antique dealers keep black lights in their stores to see the authenticity of old glass. Grace and I once shopped at one right around the corner."

Ivy and Adam entered the shop as the owner was just locking up. The bell over their heads rang. Sam kept circling the block finding it impossible to get another parking space at rush hour. In the rear of the store, under the glow of a black light, the back of the paper glowed with an address.

Back in the car, Adam told Sam, "It's an address in Arlington."

Sam looked perplexed, "If there was anything on that letter, I imagined it to be the address of the Washington Monument."

"Yeah, I thought she left us buried treasure there," Adam agreed.

"Listen up, James Bond one and two, Ms. Waters would not be digging around on government property. This is her address in Virginia. If she left anything for us, it's there."

"Don't you think that is the first place the Wildcards looked?" Sam asked.

"Don't underestimate Ms. Waters. She nearly led us on a wild chase and I'm sure she gave the Wildcards an even harder run," Ivy explained. "It won't hurt looking around."

"It's dangerous to be driving around in this car any longer, Sam," Adam told him. "There's got to be an all-points-bulletin out for us."

"I still have a horse stabled near the park that's waiting to be moved to my land. What if I use one of those buggies to hitch my Morgan to?"

"Talk about being noticed!" Adam ranted. "The cops will be all over us."

"Not really. There are horse and buggies with drivers pulling couples and families all over the city. We will blend right in and no one will think to look for us among them. I'll be the driver and you two can be the riders. Hopefully, the weather will cooperate for there's a park law that horses can't be out on the Washington streets in freezing weather."

Chapter Twenty Four

Snow had stopped. The weather in D.C. had risen to thirty-eight degrees. The fresh snow was starting to melt but it was still too cold for the horse to be out of stables for long.

The Bay Morgan horse stood quietly between the shafts of the buggy in front of Ms. Water's former residence. It was an old two-story brick, framed with corbels and capped off with a sloping roof.

"Ms. Waters lived with her sister," Ivy told them wearing the extra jacket Sam found in the stable for her.

"Seems to me this would be the first place the Wildcards would have looked for what they wanted. If for some reason they don't have it, then Ms. Waters' things might have been sold or donated by now," Sam figured.

"We won't know for sure until we have a look inside for ourselves. All along it's been everyone's contention that the missing software was either given to me by Ms. Waters or something I stole from her. Now I'm thinking it's neither. I'm quite certain it's something she told me," Ivy shivered as the cold seeped through her clothes into her bones. "The book was only a way to help remind me. Ms. Waters said she had a picture of the obelisk hanging in her townhouse."

"And you think that's where the software is? In the frame behind this picture?" Adam asked.

"I really think so. Let's see if Ms. Waters' sister

is home and if she still has the picture."

Sam secured the horse and buggy before going up the steps with Adam and Ivy. The doorbell was answered within seconds. The similarity between the woman who stood in the doorway and the murdered woman nearly knocked the wind out of them all. "Yes?" The sister looked curiously into their faces and then at the buggy in the street.

Sam pulled out his news credentials.

"Oh, so you are reporters. I recognize you, Mr. Oliver, from the evening news that I watch from time to time. I'm Christine Matthews, how may I help you?"

"We're here about your sister, Geneen Waters," Sam explained.

"Of course, you are. The wind is picking up. Come on in and let's sit by the fire." Christine led them into the living room where they seated themselves. The news was on, but Christine muted the sound.

Sam dove right in. "I understand Ms. Waters was fascinated with Egypt."

"Oh?" Christine seemed confused and played with the pearls she wore along her neckline. "I don't think so."

Sam, Adam and Ivy looked at one another with great surprise. Ivy glanced at the TV and back at Christine who had a full view of the news. Ivy then moved from where she sat in a chair to the other side of the room, next to Christine on the couch. "Ms. Waters gave me a book on the first Lady Pharaoh of Egypt."

"Then you knew my sister." Christine seemed pleased and patted her arm.

Ivy caught hold of her hand but cut the details short. "Yes, we worked together at the White House. She told me she had a picture of an Egyptian obelisk that was hung here in the townhouse."

"A what?" Christine seemed more confused.

"It's shaped like the Washington Monument," Sam explained.

"Oh, yes, there was a picture like that in her room but it was destroyed during the robbery. It was really awful. During my sister's funeral, there was a break-in here at the house. The police said it's common for these kinds of things to happen. Crooks peruse the paper for funerals and then when the family is at church grieving, in they come."

"Was anything taken?" Adam asked.

"That's the strange thing, nothing was taken, but the place was messed up. Thank the good Lord for insurance."

"Where is the picture now?" Ivy asked.

"I tossed it. The picture was in shreds."

"You've been wonderful help." Sam abruptly got to his feet. "We are sorry about your sister's death."

"Thank you for your condolences."

On the way to the door, Ivy couldn't let it go. They had come so far and this conversation had been anything but satisfying. Ivy turned and asked, "I know this may be an imposition, but may I have a look at Ms. Waters' room?"

"Why?"

"Ms. Waters always spoke of how much she loved her home and I loved Ms. Waters." Ivy began to cry. "It would mean so much to me just to see her room."

"Of course, of course, take all the time you need." Christine stepped in front of the men to bar their way. "Geneen's room is at the end of the hall."

Ivy easily found it and turned on the light. The first thing to catch her eye was the antique vanity in the far corner. Hairbrush, comb, mirror and perfume were still laid out. Not a smidge of dust anywhere. She checked the drawers. Nothing. The wall curtains were drawn tightly together. Ivy pulled them open to a panoramic view of the Potomac River. A cornucopia of city lights burned along two shorelines.

"Ivy, are you all right?" Christine called.

"Yes, I'm fine. Just a few more minutes!" Ivy turned from the window and caught the toe of her shoe on an oriental rug. The stumble made her look up toward an odd shaped column. It was an obelisk, used as an architectural element in the room. Built just outside the closet, it was hardly noticeable. If it hadn't been for all the talk about Egyptian design, Ivy wouldn't have given it a thought. The column was painted the same color as the bedroom walls. The crown molding seemed to be gold leaf. Ivy frantically began to knock on all sides of the column. If she was correct about the package being hidden inside, there'd be a hollow spot. She found it near the base. Down on her knees, she pushed hard on the place until a small trap door sprang open. Ivy sucked a deep breath knowing the answers were finally within her reach.

Ivy peered inside and saw a large package. She plunged her hand into the opening and grabbed a hold. She tugged and tugged. Finally out it came; a large padded envelope with her name written in bold letters. She tucked the envelope inside her jacket. Before she left the room, she closed the compartment. Now with the composure of a queen, Ivy walked to the front door where everyone was idly talking about how good Christmas cookies were.

"Thank you, Ms. Matthews, and again, I am so sorry about Ms. Waters." Ivy swiped a tear from the corner of her eye. "I loved your sister."

On the steps of the townhouse, Ivy, Adam and Sam stood near a window where they had a straight shot of seeing into the living room. They watched as Christine picked up the control and sat down to watch the news.

"In a few minutes, our faces are going to be on that screen as wanted by the FBI. How long do you think it will take her to make the call?" Adam asked.

"Seconds. She's reaching for the phone now," Ivy said standing on her tiptoes.

They ran down the steps to the buggy. Adam helped Ivy into the carriage as Sam climbed into the driver's seat. Adam noted, "In actuality, she could have been ordering take-out."

It was then they heard the far off whines of sirens.

"That doesn't mean they're coming for us," Adam glanced around. "Not when there's a city full of crime."

Sam picked up the reins and gave the Morgan a nudge with the crop. "I hope you're right. Driving a horse-drawn buggy isn't exactly a great get-away vehicle."

A few blocks down, they turned a corner and went down two more streets before stopping under a grove of trees near a park. The sirens were getting closer.

"We can try to hide here but I think we'll be easily discovered."

Triumphantly, Ivy pulled out her treasure. She held up the large envelope thick with information. "I think I've found Ms. Waters' treasure. If I'm right, we do not want to get caught with this on us."

Sam reached under his seat and took out a solar lantern. The light cast a green shadow over them. Ivy handed the envelope to Adam. "Here is what you have spent the last eight years searching for."

Adam refused. "The honor goes to you, Ivy."

Eagerly, Ivy tore open the top of the envelope. Her stomach tumbled when she looked inside. It was all bundled up together. The three of them let out a collective gasp. With great care Ivy slowly pulled out software, plans, names, dates, and social security numbers. And the prototype. On the top of the pile was the name *Top Dog Boss.* Ivy passed the items around to Adam and Sam. They sat in silence as they looked through the information.

"After all this time, Adam, here it is. Your case is right here."

"Ms. Waters left Ivy all the clues to find where they had been hidden," Sam said.

"But who is Top Dog Boss?" Adam asked just as his cell phone rang. He turned it off without looking at the caller.

Ivy began counting out the letters to the name. "Top Dog Boss. It has the right number of digits to be a phone number."

"Let's try it." Adam took his cell back out and punched in the letters carefully. It rang three times. "Hello."

"It's me," Adam spoke cryptically.

"Try speaker phone, so we can listen," Sam whispered.

Speakerphone on.

"Identify yourself."

"The software has been located," Adam said.

"Where?"

Adam covered the mouthpiece with his fingers. "His voice is so familiar but I just can't place it." He uncovered it and answered. "Details are given only in person."

"Then we are ready to meet."

"I am at your service."

"Goodie gun drops." The voice crooned.

Ivy's eyes lit up in recognition. She searched the pockets of the jacket she wore and came up with a pen. She wrote on her hand *Grayson* and held it up.

Adam quickly covered the mouthpiece again. "Are you sure?"

"Grayson says goodie *gun* drops not goodie *gum* drops. It's him. Top Dog is the Vice President.

There's something that doesn't make sense to me," Ivy began. "What we now have in our possession is about Presidential campaigns. How does an unpopular, low-sitting congressman fit into this?"

"It's Gram's brainchild. He designed it and he is the test model—the guinea pig. The wildcard will be waiting in the wings to sweep the election at the last minute."

"And now we know who Top Dog is," Ivy added.

By now, they could see red flashing lights streaming over the bridge from Washington into Arlington. More sirens came from the west.

"Interference Top Dog. I'll call back." He flipped the phone closed, turning it off as he did, and shoved the cell back into his pocket. Sirens continued to whine in their direction. The sky quickly became a profusion of sirens and lights, including an FBI helicopter with searchlights.

"We're pretty well hemmed in," Sam worried.

"It's like the Wildcards are being unleashed on us."

"It's a good way to lose this information forever," Adam said. "We need to split up."

"No," Sam protested.

"Sam, he's right. Adam, you take the envelope and go," Ivy insisted as she put all the information back into the envelope.

"Ivy, I can't leave you." Adam looked at her intently.

"Sure you can," Sam said. "Ivy and I will lead them away from you."

"It's the only way." Ivy stepped over the back of the front seat and plopped down beside Sam. She handed the envelope to Adam and took Sam's arm.

Adam looked from Sam to Ivy. "Ivy…I can't leave you here, not you either, Sam."

"Who's thinking with their emotions now?" Ivy snapped. "Get going!"

"I'll come for you both. Sam, make sure you keep our girl safe." Adam jumped down from the buggy and ran through the trees heading in the direction of the river.

Sam and Ivy waited quietly together for the inevitable. "Sam, what are your dreams?"

He seemed startled over her question. "What an odd question to ask at a time like this. We're about to be arrested by the Feds."

"We may not get another chance to talk for a long time. So please humor me and answer my question."

Sam sighed heavily and finally answered, "Dreams are impractical."

"What? This comes from a man who bought me a music box?"

"You picked it out."

Ivy had forgotten. "You once told me you were born to grant all my dreams."

Sam snorted, "I couldn't have. That is the hokiest thing I have ever heard." He gave the reins a slap and pulled out onto the street, turning the horses in the direction of the townhouse. Suddenly, they became trapped in a flood of lights.

Chapter Twenty-Five

The jail door opened at Quantico.

"Ivy…" Eyes and smile.

"You sure took your sweet time," Ivy grumbled at Adam as she hopped down from the bunk. But as always, she couldn't remain mad at him. She crossed over to his arms.

"I've come to take you home, Ivy Dillon." Adam kissed her forehead.

"Where's Sam?"

"Sam? This is the first time you've seen me in a week and all you can think to ask me is about Sam? Well, darling, Sam is his way back to Washington." Adam lost his smile. His professional aura returned. "Just follow me."

Ivy couldn't get over how Sam could have left without waiting for her. They all had been in this together. Well, never mind about Sam. She pulled on Adam's arm. "Adam, I'm sorry. Please take me home."

Adam wrapped his arms around her and sighed deeply into her hair. "Before I do, someone wants to see you."

"Who? If it's Rob, I can't do it."

"It's not Rob. Trust me. You'll want to see this person." They stopped in front of a metal door. "I'll be right here waiting if you need me. Go on in. The prisoner will be here in a minute."

The walls inside the room were a drab green. A metal table with chairs was the only furniture. In the far corner of the room was a window with blinds pulled all the way up so she could see it was still snowing. Snow had come to Washington. When this case first started, it had been spring with cherry blossoms.

She sat at the table to wait. Jittery nerves, jittery feet...heels and toes, heels and toes, her feet fretfully danced under the table. The door opened. A woman in a jumpsuit walked in. Erin's wrists were handcuffed and her legs were in shackles. She took the seat, opposite Ivy.

"A hundred times I've imagined us sitting just like this having this conversation, but somehow I thought we'd be at a trendy restaurant with a dulcimer playing in the background. Like that place just off M Street." Erin seemed relaxed.

"It's a good place to eat." Ivy agreed, not sure how to react.

"You know, I will really miss those little round tables that dot the room with waiters scurrying about with silver trays of food. You'll have to go for me and tell me about it. That way I can live vicariously through you," Erin shook her head as if wondering how she ended up here.

"Erin, did you have anything to do with Ms. Waters' murder?"

"No, I didn't, but there are a lot of things you don't know or understand about me, or Rob for that matter. The Feds now know, and I wanted to be the one to explain it to you. It's better if you hear it from me." Erin tapped nervously on the tabletop with her recently trimmed nails. The handcuffs clattered.

"I'm listening."

"The events that took place on the night of the charity ball have shaped my life. When I close my eyes, I can imagine the water along the shore of the Yacht Club. Rob and Tony had a trunk filled with bottles of really good Bourbon. We took a couple of bottles out and went down to the lake to drink them.

We told really crazy, silly stories, but Rob's was the best. It was the craziest of all. He told us about this radical political course at college and got the idea that the American people's votes could be bypassed with rigging voting machines. In his desperation to control the American policy, he decided to run for office, starting with congress, and find someone to build him a prototype so he could make it to president. Imagine, our elected public officials determined by someone manipulating a few electrical impulses. Evidently, he had a computer genius who said he could build him a prototype but it would cost him a lot of money. That's why we took the money from the charity ball that night."

"That explains where the money went and the motive for the robbery, but what about Karin?"

"Ah, Karin. She caught us stealing the money and was going to turn us in. We pushed her into the car, drove her around the lake trying to talk to her out of it." Erin's eyes were as dead as a winter root. "I guess that was the beginning of the end for me. My fate was sealed when she drown."

"How could you hate your very own sister?"

Erin looked surprised at Ivy's comment. "I didn't hate Karin. I simply felt nothing for her. Poor Karin, she looked so scared. Her eyes were like round saucers when we pulled her down to the lake, and by the way, you were right, it was the Illinois side. I used to love playing with your mind. Anyway, Rob blocked the way when she tried to run from us. So then she tried to swim away from us, but Karin couldn't swim. We sat on the beach and watched as she struggled in the water. Sometimes, I can still hear the bubbles as her body sunk. When she disappeared, we made a toast. Anyway, we had to create an illusion so people would think she had run off with the money. It was Rob's idea."

"You didn't try to save her?"

"It was over pretty fast. I don't think she suffered much," Erin said this like it would make Ivy feel better.

"Were you in contact with Rob from that point on?"

"Oh no. We made a pledge together that night to keep both secrets—the money and Karin's death. The next time I heard from Rob was when I was at state college majoring in Theater Arts. Rob was getting ready to run for congress and wanted to be sure I wasn't talking." She sat quietly for a few moments. "If Rob hadn't walked back into my life, I would never have sought him out. I think watching Karin die formed this bond between us and he was somehow driven to see me again, and again, and again. He ruined all the relationships I had with men from then on."

"So Rob contacted you again in college?" Ivy tried to move the story along.

"Yes. Rob said he had connections to finance an independent political paper. People outside the college would run it. However, to be sure the University wouldn't ban the paper, it had to appear to come from students, so that is where I came in. I was to be the editor in name only. It was Rob's feeble way of starting into politics by disrupting the way people thought about present elections. He hoped it would create enough attention to spread across the nation. Agent Bennett soon joined our team, although he used another name at that time. The paper failed about the same time we discovered Bennett was working undercover. I graduated and moved away, but Bennett had a way of popping up now and again pressuring me to go undercover for him. I wanted to be left alone so I legally changed my name. He always seemed to find me. I didn't realize Rob was trying to find me, too."

"When did you reconnect with him?"

"When I went to Chicago to audition. The rest you know."

"And in Washington, Adam was the 'Voice'?"

"He told you! Yes, Adam was the 'Voice' and he sure scared me. I was caught between Rob and the Wildcards and Bennett so I kept changing apartments and phone numbers."

"And when did you and Rob decide to marry?"

"When you left Chicago for the north woods, I went after Rob. I told him if you ever found out about how Karin died, you'd turn him in. He knew what I said was true. It was only a matter of time until you discovered the truth."

Adam walked into the room for Ivy, when the guard came for Erin. Ivy looked up at him. "Just another minute, Adam, please." At his nod, she turned back to Erin. "I know I should be angry with you, Erin, but somehow I just can't be. I don't understand what you have done and probably never will."

"Good-bye, Ivy." Erin turned and walked out.

****

Ivy sat beside Adam on the plane ride home. It was her first time ever in First Class. They ate cheese and crackers and drank sparkling wine, snuggling into one another. Just before the plane landed, Adam told her, "I won't be staying. I need to get back to Washington but wanted to see you at least part way home. Your father is meeting us at O'Hare and will drive you back to Twin Lakes. Ivy, there's something you need to know about your mother."

****

Ivy was still digesting the news Adam had shared. Being with her father helped as he took her to her mother's final resting place. It should have been overcast, but it was an unexpectedly sunny, blue-sky day. The early October leaves tumbled this way and that, being pushed along by a wintry wind.

Ivy stood with her father by her mother's grave. She had passed away quietly in her sleep from a stroke months before the case ended. Time had been stolen from her. People had been taken from her. Ivy's lips trembled when she read the headstone—*Beloved Wife and Mother. You Are With Us Still.* She laid the bouquet of flowers on the granite marker. She glanced up at her dad who was wiping tears from his eyes.

He sniffled hard. "Ready to go?"

"Almost. Before we leave, there's one more grave I want to visit."

He nodded. "I'll meet you back at the car. Take your time."

Ivy watched her father walk back to the car and get in before she turned in another direction. From the pine trees, she took the footpath to her friend's grave. It had been recently tended to with a fresh planting of fall flowers. Ivy was glad she wasn't forgotten.

"Karin, it's been a long time. I've been on quite an adventure this past year and a half. I know everything now, how you died and why. Remember when you led me to the Lord at your church during that tent revival? You knelt beside me and taught me not to be ashamed of my feelings. I haven't exactly taken the easy road with my life but I did have lots of the Lord's help along the way. I hope I am a little better at following him from here on out. I'm glad I knew you." Ivy brushed a tear away. "Erin is so lost, Karin. I wanted to give up, wash my hands of her and walk away but then I thought of you. I thought of how you'd never give up, so I won't either. I love you, Karin, and miss you."

Ivy rose and touched the marker one last time. Funny how it could almost seem warm even in this cold weather. "Thank you, Lord, for a friend like

Karin." Ivy turned and hurried back down the path and across the brown grass. The wind had picked up causing the midmorning air to chill even more. Small sparrows collected on the ground, hopping about, and as she approached, they took to the air, soaring fragments against the blue. Ivy turned and looked at the edge of the road where her dad waited.

"Let's go home, Dad. Sam starts his national report about the Wildcards at noon."

"There's still time for one more stop. I promise to make it a quick one."

Her dad put the car in gear. The cemetery's small road was bumpy with ruts making it impossible to drive more than fifteen miles an hour. Once on the main road, he accelerated as Ivy looked at the passing barns and farmhouses. With harvest well over, farmers were repairing snow fences in patchy fields to help hold back the brutal snowstorms which were sure to come. "Where are we going?"

"You'll see." He turned onto the road where she and Sam once planned to live. It seemed a lifetime ago, a time when they were very different people. Why was her dad taking her to the yellow house today of all days? Her cup was running over with emotion, and she was quite sure she couldn't withstand much more. She prayed the house hadn't been knocked down to make way for a strip mall; it would be too hard to bear. All she wanted to do now was go home and watch the news, and hope for a call from Adam. Since his return to Washington, his calls were infrequent and left her feeling lonelier than she could ever remember.

She noticed the pine trees had grown taller and fuller since the last time she was here. Nice shelter for the birds and small wildlife in all seasons. The gravel made popping noises as the tires rolled over them before coming to a stop. There it was. To her delight, the yellow house remained but with a fresh coat of buttery-colored paint. Black shutters hung on either side of all the windows. The porch had been nicely repaired and was painted a soft white.

Ivy pulled open the car door and got out; she stood with her hands on her hips looking about the well-maintained property. Her dad asked, "Did you read the sign?"

Ivy turned and read, *'Welcome to Karin's Haven'.*

"It's a hospice house."

"But I thought you and Mom sold this place over a year ago."

"We did. Sold it to the state but Sam Oliver bought it back and dedicated this to the memory of your friend. It should be ready to open by spring."

"Sam did this?"

"It seems a lot has changed around here in Twin Lakes."

"I never would have imagined any of it." Ivy blinked back tears.

"Come on, let's go home so we can see Sam on the news. Can't wait to hear about how you saved America."

"Dad, I didn't save America."

"That's not how the folks here in town see it. Me either."

"Fine, maybe someone will hire me then. I still need a job."

Chapter Twenty-Six

Anchorman Sam Oliver was breaking the biggest story of his career.

All the stations were carrying a marathon newscast. Sam was in the first hour of a ten-hour broadcast complete with video. Starting with the Charity Ball at the Yacht Club on Lake Mary, Sam walked the viewers through the story. At times, video showed the different locations. He told of Karin's death followed by a nameless Washington intern who, along with Ms. Geneen Waters, overheard a deadly conversation.

"Ivy, what do you want to eat?" Paul stood in the kitchen doorway. "There's that macaroni and cheese from last night's dinner I can reheat for us."

"That'll be fine," she answered.

"I also have some hot dogs. I can throw those in, too."

"Yum." Ivy felt chilly and went to the closet for a sweater. Up on the top shelf was the music box. Her mother saved it for her after all. Ivy placed the music box on the table just as a car door slammed at the front of the house. Ivy peered out the window and got to the door before the bell rang. There stood Adam. He carried her laptop into the house. "I remembered how important your laptop is to you so I thought I would personally deliver it." He set it down on the living room table next to the music box.

"Adam, I've missed you!" Ivy felt giddy to see him.

"I was hoping I'd be missed."

"Oh boy, were you missed." She went in for a kiss but he dodged her.

"By the way, do you need a job?"

"Maybe." Ivy arched an eyebrow. "Why?"

"I need a good partner." He drew in a long breath, savoring the moment.

"I'd be working for you?" Ivy stepped toward Adam.

"Yes, or for the President." Adam stepped back playfully.

"The President?"

"That's why I'm here. Well, one of the reasons I'm here." Adam handed her an official envelope with the Presidential stamp on it. Her name was handwritten on the front.

It was an invitation for her to be trained as a secret service agent and upon completion of the program to serve the President of the United States. "What do I do? What do I say?"

"You tell one of us 'yes' and pass on the other offer. I assure you working with me will be so much more interesting." Adam winked. He waited for her answer. She loved watching him wait. She loved watching him. She loved watching. She loved. She...*I love Adam.*

Adam cleared his throat, "Before you answer, there is something you need to know. Back in Quantico, I left you with a misconception about Sam."

"Oh?"

"You asked where Sam was and I said he was on his way back to Washington. That part is true but before he left, he asked about you. I told him you had already left for home."

"Why would you tell him that?"

"Sam is a good guy, but he had his chance with you and blew it when he married someone else. I didn't want you running into his arms when you belong in mine. Ivy, I love you."

"Adam, there is something you need to know."

"I don't think I like the sound of that." Adam shook his head.

"Sam and I..."

Adam caught sight of the music box on the table and pressed the lever. It began playing the light airy music. They listened for a few minutes before it wound down. "Wow, I haven't heard that song for a long time."

"Adam, do you know the name of it?" Ivy held her breath and looked him in the eyes.

"My mother used to sing it to me as her mother once sang it to her, and her mother before her. It was a popular song in the early 1900s."

"Adam, what is the name?"

"The name of the song is *Tell Me Your Dreams And I Will Tell You Mine*."

Sam Oliver suddenly looked up at the screen and smiled. He seemed to smile just for her, although she knew that was impossible. Ivy heard his voice inside her head, *when you find out the name to the song then your life will be as it should.*

Now those same words echoed clearly into her heart and she heard its true meaning. Her life was exactly as it should be, and it wasn't with Sam. Adam didn't understand any of it as he stepped in front of Ivy to block her view of Sam. Her hands trembled as she reached for the remote and shut the TV off. Shut off Sam and his voice. Adam had to hear what she had to say.

"Tell me your dreams and I will tell you mine..." Ivy echoed. "Tell me, Adam, do you believe in dreams?"

"Of course. Sometimes a dream is all I have." Adam looked at her with longing and then kissed both her cheeks. "Like the dream I have of marrying you."

"Marrying me? You want to marry me? Really?" She searched for her answer in his face. When she realized this wasn't a joke, her hand fluttered to her heart that spun faster.

"Yes, really. You inspire me. I never knew that I could love anyone the way I love you." Tears swamped Adam's eyes. "From the day, we rode together in the backseat of the limo toward Chicago, I became one hundred percent committed to you."

Ivy stood on her tiptoes and kissed him.

"I have something for you." Adam reached into his pocket and pulled out a small gray velvet box, opened it and then turned it around for her to see.

It was eerily familiar. A large ruby set in the center of the 14K gold band, reminiscent of the first ring Adam had given to her and therefore highly suspicious.

"I designed the ring." Adam was smiling.

"You sure did." She sucked in her breath. "Is there a GPS under the stone?" she asked arching an eyebrow. "I have visions of myself out shopping and all of a sudden you show up."

"Would that be so terrible?"

"No, I think it'd be lovely. You could help carry all my packages home."

"Actually, there is a surprise tied in with the ring but not the one you think. Go ahead and look."

"You've raised my curiosity." Determined, Ivy tried finding the spring on the stone that would open up the small compartment. The stone didn't budge, but just as she suspected, there was something. It was an inscription that ran around the inside of the band. The circle of words read, *Dream along with me, the best is yet to be.*

"I'm still waiting for your answer." Adam taped his foot.

"Time and again, you have told me to use my head and not emotions. However, there is a lot to be said for emotions. Right now, I am riddled with emotions. Once in life, a gal gets lucky. I did when I met you at that party."

"And I knew an angel when I saw one."

"Of course, I'll marry you. I do love you, Adam." Her voice cracked.

"Finally, you said those words! I have waited a long time but it's been worth it. Let me put this ring on your finger and we'll tell your dad we're going to have a wedding. I want to declare my love to you in front of whole world."

"Spoken like a true FBI man." Ivy patted him. Turning a bit wistful, she added, "I just wish my mom was here."

"I have a feeling she knows." Adam leaned in to whisper in her ear, "Ivy, tell me your dreams, my dearest love, so I can grant them—each and every one." Then he stared at her with his superb green eyes, but it was his slow smile that pierced her heart. Eyes and smile. Together they pulled her into a sea of wild imaginations. It was meant to be.

A word about the author...

Robin Shope is a Special Education Coordinator at a county school for at risk kids by day and a romance/mystery writer by night. Holding four certifications in education, Robin is a former missionary and a pastor's wife. She has been married for over thirty years and has two grown children.

To date, her popular literary works include approximately two hundred articles in magazines such as Live, Lookout, Mennonite, Christian Reader, Decision, and Breakthrough. Other short stories appear in the books A Match Made in Heaven, Stories from the Heart, The Evolving Woman, and in the New York Times bestseller, In The Arms of Angels by Joan Wester-Anderson. Ann Spangler also used one of Robin's stories in her book, Help! I can't stop Laughing. Another two-dozen stories have been published in the Chicken Soup books. One story, Mom's Last Laugh, was re-enacted for a PAX-TV program It's a Miracle. Robin co-authored a thriller, The Chase, and her second book, The Replacement, was released in June 2006. Robin completed her third book, The Candidate, which was a 2007 release. Wildcard is Robin's fourth book, but her first with The Wild Rose Press.

Thank you for purchasing
this Wild Rose Press publication.
For other wonderful stories of romance,
please visit our on-line bookstore at
www.thewildrosepress.com.

For questions or more information,
contact us at info@thewildrosepress.com.

The Wild Rose Press
www.TheWildRosePress.com

www.ingramcontent.com/pod-product-compliance
Lightning Source LLC
La Vergne TN
LVHW050626100826
845148LV00011B/1753

9781601544872